THERE'S PLENTY OF ROOM IN THE MISSISSIPPI

This book is a work of fiction. Any names, places or events that resemble reality are strictly coincidental.

I hope you enjoy this book as much as I enjoyed writing it. William, Joshua, Frank and the boys invite you to come back to Dalston. There is more to come.

"There's plenty of room in the Mississippi." The words rang out as if someone had just let go of both barrels in the room. It was not so much how loud he spoke, and there wasn't a threatening tone in his voice.

I hung my head low and took the last drink of my whiskey before turning away from the bar to face the man that had silenced the rowdiest bar in town.

"It's been sixteen years since I've heard them words come out of your mouth," I said.

Now I've never known William to be startled or surprised by anything. Turns out, pa was right when he taught me that a calm man would live longer. When William caught a glance of the star on my chest, no one in the place would've thought we came up together in this hard world. You see most of the folks in Dalston were newcomers that were originally headed west, and got to our small town on the big river and stayed. That being said, they all knew I was sheriff and had all heard that phrase he spoke in a dozen or more stories. Little did most of them know, the stories were true.

It seemed like an eternity and I swear you could hear the second hand on my pocket watch tick by as everyone took in the scene before William spoke.

"Never figured on you wearing one of those," he said.

"Never thought you'd come back," I replied with a half a smile.

William spun around and tossed a silver dollar on the table and spoke to the man he obviously had been cross with. "That's for the trouble," he said calmly. "I'm not in the mood to drag your hide down to the river tonight but if you ever accuse me of cheating again, I will."

"Mister," the stranger struggled to get the words out as he wiped the sweat from his face. "You keep your dollar. I was in the wrong and I was on my way out of town anyway."

My name is Joshua Mack. I have been sheriff in Dalston for the better part of twelve years. This came as quite a surprise to William.

"How long has it been old friend," he spoke low as not to draw any more unwanted attention, "and how long since you hung that target on your vest?"

"William, it's been sixteen years like I said and I took the sheriffs job twelve years ago. It seems old man Markham wasn't fast enough when that wild Sloan bunch came through. But I was. So they offered me quarters and forty a month. Seems everything you taught me as youngsters landed me a far better job than busting broncs. What in God's name brought you back?"

"I remember the Sloans. They were a bad lot. How many did you get?"

"All three," I replied as I tapped the bar to get us a drink. "I got Ty out in the hills when he tried to shoot me in the back, but a rattler scared my horse just in time. It was a chore to get at him the way he was in the rocks waiting on me. After word got around, the other two came to town and filled Markham full of lead. I was forced to face 'em both in the street. I took three bullets but they took twelve. Guess that's why I'm telling the story."

"Now," I looked into William's eyes for the first time in ages. They were the same eyes I remembered. Eyes always tell you what kind of man you're dealing with and these eyes were hard but honest. William's eyes always reminded me of pa's eyes. Not much kindness, hardened by life, but with a straight shot of love behind them. "You never got around to telling me why you came back. You built a legend around your name, whether intentional or not, and then disappeared."

"I have some business to tend to here," he said, "and it doesn't involve you. Other than seeing how the years have treated you and knowing that my closest childhood friend turned out good, this ain't got nothing to do with you. I'll do my best to keep my affairs out of town and not cause you any trouble."

In the days of the West, the East, and everywhere that landed in between, you didn't press a man. I wanted more than my next breath to know what William was doing back in Dalston, but as long as he caused no trouble for me, it was none of my damn business. He had been born and grown here along beside me and we were the best of buds when we were young. William went to killing men at a young age, at least that's how the stories tell it. It was never pinned on him, not a single killing. Seems you can't prove a murder if there is no victim to be found.

"There's plenty of room in the Mississippi." William has used that saying since we were boys and sat on the riverbank to watch the first of the steam-powered boats pass by. He always swore that a dozen boats could pass side by side, though we never saw more than one or two at any given time, and those boats would never collide. I believe he was right. William always was right. As the years faded away, I got a job working at the Sterling Ranch and William broke and traded wild horses here and there. "No use in having to save your wages for the slow times," he would say. I didn't mind though cause pa always said a man should work for whatever he gets. William also collected and repaired old rifles and side arms for passers-by and made a piece of change that way. If he could fix the gun in a timely manner he would and if he thought it would take too long, he'd trade a dollar or two and a replacement he had previously collected and repaired, for the broken firearm. He did quite well as the folks passing through needed a weapon and most were impatient to get to the west. Seems everyone thought they'd be the next to stake a rich claim.

"Joshua," William said like he was about to deliver a speech, "I got really important business here."

I simply replied, "If you care to share the details with me, you know well that I'll help you in any way I can. I am the one with the target on my chest."

"I wish you were the only one wearing a target."

"William. If you're in trouble, maybe I can help." Will took a minute to think things over. He was a calm man.

"No. I can't ask you to be involved in this. It seems my so called past is catching up to me. I haven't been the same man since leaving Dalston all those years ago. I've tried to outrun the stories and start a new life."

"Did you leave because you were afraid of being caught?"

"I thought I told you when we were young not to believe everything you heard?"

"You did," I replied, "and it's saved me a world of trouble in my line of work."

"I'm worn out and could use a good night's rest. I just about rode my horse to death getting here. Where's the best place to get a real bed and some decent shuteye?"

"I wouldn't wish you to stay anywhere but with me. I told you they gave me quarters. William, the house is too much for a man like me."

"Joshua, I'd be happy to be your guest. Tomorrow I'll do my best to take my troubles elsewhere but it is late and I do enjoy a bed once in a while."

As I paid the tender and we turned for the door, a man stepped into the room through the swinging doors. He was almost as big as all outside. He had the worn look of any cowboy that had ridden all day and night to get where he was going and he did not look pleased to do it. He walked within twelve feet of William and stopped like he found just what he'd been searching for. I knew trouble when I saw it.

"Heard you are the fastest man this side of Bonnie." The man's words blasted across the room. By this time, every gent in the joint had backed out of the line of fire. No man wants to die in a fight that ain't his.

"I heard that too, but I never met The Kid so I wouldn't know." William smiled a little like maybe he and Billy had crossed paths and decided they should let well enough alone. The stranger did not smile. He looked as if he had never smiled. Maybe he wasn't able to.

"Care to find out," the stranger said.

"Well, seeing as how you're asking, I'm guessing that you don't know. I'd bet my best horse and my gun that you've never even been to New Mexico."

The newcomer was fast, but he wasn't sudden. That's the only way I know to describe William's hand. It was sudden. He put four in an area a queen of hearts would cover and was reloading from his belt before the man hit the floor. He fetched the dead man's gun belt and boots and gently set them on a nearby table. He then checked the man's pockets. Inside he found identification and eight dollars. William handed the belongings to me and instructed me to get them to his nearest relative.

"I've never heard his name, much less have I ever had issue with him. I guess I'm going to see how the river's running," William said, like his mother just gave him chores to do and he couldn't come out and play. Then he did what every man in the room was afraid of. He picked up the dead man's body, put him on a horse outside, and headed for the Mighty Mississippi.

CHAPTER II

In any saloon, in any town anywhere, on any given night there was always the possibility of gunplay and death. That was just the way of the west. The difference tonight in my town, and in this saloon, is the legend that was built around William's signature line. I don't believe he ever intended to be a known man. He certainly had no intentions of being sought out by every gun-toting man that thought he had something to prove. Pa and William always said, that a man with something to prove to the world had better prove to be fast. Seems no one was as fast as Will.

"Why he's not really gonna throw that man in the Mississippi is he?" The question came from a young blonde man in the corner. He looked like he just stepped off the days' last ferry.

An old timer that sat in the corner and was ignored most times replied, "Boy, unless you wanna dig a hole tonight, then damn right he is. Do you? Do you want to go dig a hole?"

"Well no I guess I don't. It just doesn't seem just for a man to dispose of a body that way. You allow that around here Sheriff?" That youngster appeared mighty nervous asking that question.

The old timer spoke up again before I could respond. "Boy, don't you ever question our Sheriff's decisions. Aside from me, he's been in this town longer than anybody. He runs things just fine if you ask me."

"I didn't ask you old man. Why don't you watch your step before I get angry."

Now to most folks, Frank Mathias was just an old man that didn't say much, but I had learned long ago that Frank was not a man to test. He came off his chair and knocked over both tables separating him and that kid quicker than anyone could move. The blonde boy's hand was dropping to his gun but when his hand reached leather, it was Frank's leathery hand, not his holster. Frank held the man's gun in place with one hand and slapped him with the other. No man wanted to cry. Getting hit that fast and that hard, left the boy with no choice.

"You listen here, you little Philadelphia punk. You came off the boat thinking you were tough but you ain't. You had better learn real quick that the west didn't move to you, you moved to it. You best figure it out real quick or you'll wind up in a hole yourself," Frank meant it too.

He let the kid go and returned to his whiskey at his table. The young man wiped his eyes and reached into his pocket to pay his tab. He wanted to leave the room. Hell, he wanted to leave town and head back east where he might have been a tough man, something inside the man told him he couldn't leave the bar and still retain his dignity. I walked over to his table with a fresh glass and offered it to him. He swallowed the whiskey as I sat down.

"Frank came up the hard way," I said. "He's been here long enough to know a man just by looking n his eyes. He's the type of man that will whip you and shake your hand, if you take it like a man."

The boy's voice was still shaky when he said, "I just never imagined a place where a man kills another man and throws him into a river."

"Listen son. Most people only know of William by legend. When William's father was murdered, we were both young. I'd say we were about thirteen and fourteen then. He's a year older than me. William and I dug that hole and when we had buried him and marked the grave, William had a look in his eyes that I'd never seen before, and until tonight, never again. William told me that day that there were few men he'd dig a hole for."

"Did they catch the man that murdered his father?"

"Sheriff Markham was hot on the trail of the man but never got the chance to arrest him. When he finally caught up with the man, that gent was lying across his horse with holes all in him. William was leading the horse to the river and Markham asked him why. 'Why dig another hole, sheriff? There's plenty of room in the Mississippi.' That's where it all began. I guess old man Markham saw fit to let William do as he pleased."

The young man looked up from his glass. "My name is Jim Thomas. I did just get off the boat, and Frank was right, I was tough where I'm from. I guess that doesn't make me tough here." He looked toward the corner and spoke up, "Buy you a drink Frank?"

"Yeah son, I guess I'm running low. Care to join me?" Frank replied dryly.

I left the men to their whiskey and stepped out into the night to go home. I knew William wouldn't be long and could still use a bed and a roof for the night. When I arrived at my cabin on the edge of town I stabled my horse and went inside to make coffee. William always liked coffee when he was younger, and I figured that never leaves a man.

14

CHAPTER III

"I smell coffee," William said as he opened the door.

"How'd you know this was my place Will?"

"I found the house furthest from town that was still in city limits and saw the light. When I went to put my horse in the stable, I knew I had the right place. You always had a love for a black horse. I have to say, this one is a bit better than that old black you were parading around when we were younger."

"Will, you put quite a scare into the folks in that saloon tonight. Most of them are newcomers. Hell, even our bartender, King Louis, has only been here four years."

"King Louis? What's the story behind him?"

"His name isn't Louis, and he sure ain't King of much, but he was the first to bring whiskey to St. Louis and that made him king there. He had an altercation with the sheriff there and thought it better to just leave town than earn a name. My guess is Louis is a good man to have on your side when things go down."

William found few things humorous but was amused by the man's name. "I guess a man gets a name any way he can, whether he wants it or not. The coffee's good Joshua. Strong, like I like it."

"You've made a name for yourself William. I never dreamed it would come to strangers hunting you in a saloon to try you. You did seem to be much faster than I remember."

"You get fast in sixteen years. I never put myself in the category with the men folks talk and write about but I've done what I've had to do to survive. 'Specially the last five years."

"What happened five years ago?"

"I told you my troubles were my troubles and I sure don't want you getting dragged into this. I got something to take care of and I'll be out of your town."

"William, you made your business mine by bringing it to my town. I'm the law here."

"If you must know, I'll tell you. Five years ago I was riding a trail out of Denver to do some mining in the hills. I had received a letter from Tom that he and Maggie were headed west to hopefully settle in California."

"I remember when they left. The whole town was there to see them off. Even the passers-by loved Tom and Maggie. Not long after they left, maybe a few weeks or a month, I quit hearing from them."

"There's a real good reason for that Joshua. Coming out of Denver, I saw just off the old trail I was following, a burned wagon. I checked my surroundings and rode over to see what had happened. Not ten feet from the wagon was Tom lying dead with five holes in him. Twenty more feet away, was Maggie. The man responsible had crossed the line with her before putting his last bullet in her head. I dug two holes that day. Those are the only graves that I've dug since you and I dug that one when we were kids."

"Tom and Maggie deserved a burial," I said.

"I always liked him growing up and was glad to see Maggie marry him. I guess if I had taken a different path, I would've married Maggie myself, but I didn't and she was happy with Tom. When I found them, I hadn't been in a single gunfight in two years and had done my best to try and outrun the name I had made for myself. It seemed every town I rode into, I heard fewer and fewer stories about me. The moment I saw Maggie lying in the high grass with her dress half torn off and a hole in her head, I became the man I was trying leave behind."

"Why didn't you just go to the sheriff, or marshal, and report it? You could have turned it over to the law."

"Joshua," William looked dead in my eyes, "I loved that woman like I love you. I couldn't let that go no matter how hard I tried."

"Well I can't honestly say I would have done any different. I know we took separate paths but I know we have the same principles."

"Once I buried the two of 'em, and said a few words from the good book, I started searching for anything that would lead me to the man or men responsible. I found a trail and followed. Many times in the months and years after that I thought I had it figured out only to lose the trail in a stampede or a storm. Sometimes, I even felt like giving up, but thought about what you would do and knew I had to keep going."

"I would have kept going too, Will. It's funny that you continued because of me and I would've because of you. We are a lot alike."

"We should be Joshua. We should be."

When I awoke in the morning, the smell of coffee filled the house. William always did wake before the Sun. I shook out my boots and strapped on my gun. My mind was full of questions. Questions I intended to get answers to but knew it wasn't going to be easy. William needed my help or he would not have told me the story the night before. He has never been a man to share information unless he had too. I got the strange feeling he told me why he had returned to Dalston because the men he was after may be too powerful or too many for him to handle alone. I never thought I would see the day there was anything William could not handle alone. Other than my Pa, he was the strongest man I have ever known.

I stepped into the main room of the house to find it empty, except for the hot coffee on the stove. If I knew William, he would be out on the porch watching the sky turn from gray, to yellow, and then to orange. He always did enjoy a sunrise. I poured myself a cup and tasted the coffee. It was strong, very strong.

"Mornin' William," I said as I stepped out the front door onto the porch. "I see you still love the sunrise."

William took a sip before he replied. "The sunrise is a new beginning whereas the sunset, pretty as it is, represents the end. I've been looking for a new beginning my entire life. Seems it's a lot harder to find than an ending. I have led too many men to the end and all I want now is to help a few more find the end they deserve and live out the rest of my days in peace."

I couldn't find a single word to say after a statement like that. I knew William never did want the name he got, and I knew he was a peaceful man for the most part. When we were children, him being a year older than me, he had the patience of Job showing me things and teaching me everything he knew. He could very well have been off courting girls or doing plum near anything else but he was by my side. He taught me everything Pa didn't have time to. He taught me to fish, hunt, and live off the land. He even taught me how to practice a quick draw and hit what I was aiming at. William always said that any man can be fast, but it takes a certain nerve to face another man and know what you have to do rather than think about what might happen. What might happen? That question alone has killed many a man in the West. You have to do what you have to do and leave the worry to someone else.

After a while, after the sun cleared the horizon, William said he was going to saddle his horse and scout out and around the town. He had a feeling that the men he wanted were well known and not to be suspect to the rest of the town. It would not be your average hell-raiser or rustler. If it was anyone that I knew could be trouble, he thought I would have already had it out with them. The men that would kill a man in cold blood and then have their way with a woman, before putting a bullet in her head, were careful men that would think they had everything figured out and couldn't be caught.

"I'll try not to cause any trouble or draw any attention to myself today," William said.

"I've never known you to hunt trouble William. It just seems to find you."

"What I mean is last night was not my doing. I had no idea that kid was after me. I knew I was being trailed, but never worried too much about it. That kid could follow a man well enough but he never got close enough to give himself away or put himself in danger. How could I have known it would lead to him calling me out in front of a bar full of folks?"

"There was no way for you to know, William. He was just another newcomer trying to make a name. He wanted to take down the biggest legend in this part of the West. It was a mistake, but not yours."

"It never gets easier does it? To kill a man and have to deal with the way civilized folks look at you. It just isn't easy Joshua. You should know, being sheriff and all."

"I don't know how it is for you, but it must be easier for me because I wear the badge. Sometimes I wish that you were my deputy and things were simple because who would buck a deck stacked as bad as that? You and I together running a town, that would be a sight to see."

"I have thought of that on many long rides and lonely nights. I proved what I could do with a gun when we were young and since then, I've just had to keep on proving it. It's not the kind of life I would've wished for when we were kids, but it's my life."

"Be safe William. As the law, I have duties this town needs me to perform. Please come back tonight. There's no reason for you to sleep outdoors when I have all this room."

"See you this evening Joshua."

William left promptly after our conversation. I went inside to pour myself one more cup and put out the fire in the stove. I did have duties to perform. These fine people, and some strangers and not so fine folks, needed me to keep order in Dalston. I had sworn to that and hoped like hell that William did not put me in a position to do otherwise. There are few men in this world that I would lay my badge down for. William and Frank were the only two I could think of at the time. They are the two men I have the most respect for since Pa died.

CHAPTER IV

I saddled the black and rode into town to the sheriff's office. There I hitched him, knowing he wasn't going anywhere even if I left him loose. He was a loyal horse and the best I had ever owned. This time of morning, the only people milling about were Mary, King Louis' wife who was up to gather eggs, and Ms. Kitchen. She was a young lady of maybe nineteen that had opened her own general store. She had told me when arriving in town that she needed a building to let and she had wagons full of goods coming in soon. I found her just the place, up the street from the sheriff's office, and sure enough the wagons came. Later, she told me her Ma had died of the fever back east and her father wanted to move out west to see if he could make his fortune. On the way west, her father had a problem with a few men and wound up dead. She told me that her father never was much one with a firearm and never stood a chance, but a few passersby in the town they were in, shot the men down. She swore to her father, with the last breath he ever heard from her, she would make it west of the Mississippi and set up shop. "I'll be fine Daddy," she told him.

She was fine at that. She had made her way west and settled in my town, Dalston. I will never forget the day she marched into my office and declared, "I came west with my daddy to open a store and he did not make it. I expect I will sheriff. I have wagons following me to supply a store that I hope you will help me find and keep."

She was fifteen then. She was grown up when she got here but I would not know how to start to describe how she has grown since arriving. What a woman she has become! There are two other stores in town, but they don't have anything against Ms. Kitchen. She attracts every cowboy within one hundred miles. It is a damn shame she will not sell a gun or ammunition to one. She said that after what happened to her father, she would rather not contribute to the behavior or lifestyle that was responsible for taking her father away from her. You could see it in her eyes. She was angry but on a mission to fulfill her father's dream of opening a store in the West. Besides that, I had every intention of helping her. She was the most beautiful girl I had ever met. It didn't take me long to find her a building to rent. King Louis had a building next to his saloon that he had been saving for the right tenant. One look and he knew she was the right tenant.

As I was making my morning rounds, I always stopped to see how Mary was. It seems Louis would come home almost every night and tell her all the interesting parts.

"Morning Mary," I spoke calmly, but was anxious to hear what Louis had said.

"Good morning sheriff. I heard last night was rather exciting."

"Yes ma'am I reckon it was a rather eventful night. Seems things will be rather interesting for a while," I replied.

Mary told me in a voice that sounded with sincerity, "You can always count on my Louis if you need him. He thinks highly of you and told me himself that any man you stand by, he also will stand by."

"That's a very good thing to hear Mary," I said. "I've always thought of Louis as someone I'd like to side with. Seems to me he's a man that's got a deep past behind him. Not to say he has anything to run from, just that he figures to be a little less innocent than some."

"You are correct sheriff. My Louis has quite a past that I have personally witnessed since we were both teenagers. He has never done anything to let me down or that has made me less proud of him. Louis is a strong man and left St. Louis on his own decision. The trouble there wasn't worth a killing when he knew he could bring me here and get a fresh start."

"Well, I'm gonna finish my rounds Mary," I said. "Tell Louis I will see him this evening."

"Good day sheriff."

I went from my normal conversation with Mary with a newfound sense of security about my town. Sure, I've had a good term as sheriff and have had the support of the town and its people, but I always feared the day when real trouble knocked on our door. Frank had always been there for me and I'm aware if it ever came to it, he'd be right by my side. William's return only meant the men he followed were here or passing through, but for now, the trouble was mine to share. Any man that would do what had happened to Maggie and Tom was very dangerous. It was good to know that I had Louis to count on.

I walked down to Ms. Kitchen's store to see her, like I did every morning. In the West, there are few places that smell good. Most places are full of filthy cowboys, or horses, or dust, or all of the above. For her store to always have the aroma of fresh lavender was almost a miracle. She kept the cleanest establishment in town, perhaps in the West. Every shirt was folded neatly. Every can faced forward. Everything was seemingly perfect, just like the smile on her face.

"Good morning Ms. Kitchen," I said while walking through the door and taking in a deep breath of lavender.

"Morning sheriff. Think you'll ever call me Emily?"

"Well, ma'am, I intend to someday."

"When do you think that day will come, Joshua?" She called me Joshua to help her point that formalities were wasted between us.

"Trust me , someday your name will not be Ms. Kitchen, as it was when we met, and then I shall call you Emily."

"You are a very peculiar man that sometimes makes me wonder what goes on in a head like yours. I look forward to the day you finally call me by my first name sheriff. I heard from Mary, just before you came, that a known man rode into town last night and it could spell trouble. You know well that I do not like guns or the trouble they bring." I knew she meant it.

"I understand Ms. Kitchen, and I don't like trouble either. That being said, without law and men wi ling to stand up for folks, the bad of the West would take over. I couldn't sleep at night if I didn't do my job and protect this town." I was trying my best to paint myself in a good light in her eyes and get my point across.

"Well I understand Joshua. I also believe if that small town my father died in had a sheriff half the man you are, I would not have arrived in Dalston alone."

27

I didn't have much to say to that, though it may have been true. I would do anything to help Ms. Kitchen.

"Joshua," she said, "I have a bit of work to get done before the rest of town gets stirring and I was told that there is a herd being held just outside of town."

I was just turning to leave and spun back to her. "Did you say a herd?"

"Why yes sheriff," she replied as if surprised I didn't know. "A cowboy rode in here yesterday and said he and his boss would be back in two days to get supplies and arrange a few sales before moving on. He seemed nice enough but he did wear two guns and looked tough. I thought you would already know about them."

"I got word a few months ago that one of these moving herds was headed this way but I didn't know they were already here. Thank you, Ms. Kitchen. I can always count on the prettiest girl in town to know when there are new cowboys around."

She blushed a little, taking her complement well and I made my way to the door. Once out on the boardwalk, I recalled the one trip I had made East and the way the brick sidewalks sounded under my boots. There's just nothing like an old wooden boardwalk. The click clack and feeling is like nothing you find back East.

Now I had work to do. A group of cowboys on the outskirts of town and William and his hunt were both problems I had to face. I decided that after lunch I would take a nice afternoon ride out to the camp of the herd and introduce myself as sheriff. My job was the town. I had no jurisdiction outside, but maybe I could get a feel as to what type of men I was dealing with.

CHAPTER V

William left the house on the edge of town and rode due north. East was no way to go, unless he was headed to the river. I was hoping to reduce the number of trips William made to the Mississippi to as few as possible. By now, we all knew why he went there. To the south was the Sterling Ranch that I had worked for as a younger man. William knew old man Sterling and was even offered a job on the ranch many times before becoming the legend he was. William had come from the west of town and I well knew that if his man was there, he may have taken care of his business and turned back for Colorado or anywhere else. William never was much for the past. It was good to see him though. I miss those days as kids by the river watching the steamboats go by. I couldn't help thinking maybe when everything was settled, William and I could go watch the boats again; just like when we were young.

William mentioned nothing of a herd. If it was west, he would have seen it, and knowing I was sheriff, he would have told me. I knew nobody would bring a herd in from the south for the chance of crossing Sterling's place. Separating cattle from a herd and a ranch is not a task anyone would be anxious to undertake. The herd had to be north of town and that made sense that a herd would go to St. Louis first. A bigger town means more sales. These boys would be trying to rid themselves of any leftovers they may have before heading back home, wherever that may be. It dawned on me all of a sudden, William rode north.

When I approached the camp, I could hear laughter and William's big voice carrying over it. William had a way with a story and was easy to get along with, as long as no one knew the legend behind him and tried to test him. He always commanded respect. Pa used to say, "That's the problem with most men boy, they demand respect, deserved or not, rather than commanding it. If a man carries himself as a man and expects others to do the same, he can command a certain respect." I missed Pa more and more when I thought of such things, though he'd been gone for years.

"Permission to ride into camp," I shouted once I was in close enough range.

"We seen you coming for a while," a short skinny man holding a lever action rifle replied. "If we was worried 'bout you, you wouldn't have made it this far."

I rode up and got down from the big black. I loosened the girth on my saddle and let the horse go. These boys looked at me like I was crazy and I turned to say, "He ain't going nowhere. He knows I need a ride home."

One man snickered at the comment and I noticed that William had moved from the center of the group as if he was preparing for trouble. When I walked closer to the cook fire, all the men got restless. You would've thought I was carrying a rattler towards them. It didn't occur to me until a portly man stood up and pointed it out that I was wearing my badge.

"We don't like lawmen coming around trying to tell us what's what mister," he said.

"Well good," I said firmly. "I don't have any power in these parts. My job stops at the city limits. I just wanted to get to know the type of men I would be dealing with when y'all come to my town. I didn't ride all this way to try and throw my weight around. I just like to be prepared." I said it all with a certain calmness that one develops after being sheriff for so long.

"Maybe one newcomer riding in," the wiry man that didn't take his hand far from his holster said, "is enough for one day. Just maybe we don't want no more company. Maybe we don't like badges and I should shoot that one off your chest!"

Just as he started to continue down maybe lane, and had opened his mouth one too many times for my liking, I pulled leather. Now I may not be William, but you don't remain in charge of a town for as long as I have in the West without being good at what you do. When I reached for my gun, the wiry little mouth of a man also went to drawing. When I had my pistol pointed at his heart by the time he was just raising his, you could smell the fear in him. He hesitated.

"I told you I got no power here, but I'll be damned if you'll threaten my life anywhere," I said it softly for you could have heard a fly land at that moment

"I was just testing you mister. I meant no harm," he said.

"I've been tested for twelve years wearing this badge, and obviously I passed all of 'em. Next time you feel like administering a test, you better choose a subject that needs it. I came in peace and would like very much to leave that way." I hadn't been this riled since the Sloans.

I heard the click of the hammer behind me before I heard the voice. "Well I reckon you may be fast, but this is my outfit and I don't like when a man draws on one of my boys. You turn around real slow."

34

I was scared. I haven't had the opportunity to admit that many times in my life, for most things happen so fast I didn't have time to be scared, but right then I was. I turned slowly. No wonder he was the boss. He was a big powerful man, with a smoothness about his voice and the way he stood. This was not a man I wanted to upset, though it seemed too late for that. Just as I was wondering if I'd get out of this alive, I saw William sitting on his horse and then the men were properly introduced to the man they had just been laughing with.

"If you don't drop that pistol," he roared like a lion I had seen in a circus once back East, "you're boys will be deciding who's in charge tonight. The man said he came in peace and your man prodded him. If your man hadn't been so slow, we wouldn't be having this conversation but turns out that old Joshua Mack, the sheriff there, is faster than I remember."

"We got no problems with you cowboy," the foreman said as he held his gun on me and the rest of his crew, all twenty of them, stood still to see the next move. I don't reckon anyone ever put their boss in his place before because they were stunned.

He was quite a sight. Most men would prefer to shoot from the ground but William knew the importance of the intimidation he was portraying by being mounted. The high ground holds importance as does the fact that none of them wanted to risk being shot by a man already atop a horse. He could ride away at his leisure. He had a scattergun in one hand, a pistol in the other and his rifle across his lap. I well knew at that moment that if these men had the sense the Good Lord gave them, I was going to ride away just fine.

William said the words louder than I've ever heard him speak. "If lead starts flying, men start dying. By that, I mean you mister. You will die first and your horse will be tired tonight from carrying you to the river. There's plenty of room in the Mississippi!"

The men, like a chorus, all took a deep breath. They realized at that point that it may very well be their last breath. Legend traveled faster than a telegram in the West. Everybody knew when The Kid killed somebody. Everyone knew about the Earps. Everyone, and I mean everyone, knew what the words William said meant.

"Well I'll be damned," the foreman said. "You're William Mack. A man with a story and a gun perhaps bigger than the whole outdoors. Why didn't you say that's who you were? Why are you, of all people, defending this sheriff?"

William never let down his guard. He spoke calmly, "You just said it yourself. My name is William Mack. His name is Joshua Mack. Why don't you put two and two together and drop that gun. That is the only way this ends well for you. I've never killed nobody that didn't have it coming and my brother, I am certain, is a fair and just sheriff in Dalston. If he said he comes in peace then by God let there be peace. Otherwise you better hope your ghost can swim."

The foreman dropped his gun slowly to the ground and kicked it a few feet away. His men were tense and knew they had to follow the lead of their foreman. At the very moment he dropped his weapon, they all followed suit and moved their hands slowly from their holsters. All but one that is. There was one man on the edge of the group with his hand hovering over his pistol. He had a very wry look on his face and perhaps even a half a smile. It appeared that he may draw at any given moment on any little whim. I looked over at the man; a look of uncertainty was in his eyes.

"Mister it appears that you are the only man here trying to cause trouble," I said loudly.

"I just ain't sure if you and William there can take me before I can take you," the man said.

The foreman replied before William or I could. "Damn it Pike, even you ain't that fast. Can't you see these boys got control here and by God if William Mack and his brother, the sheriff, say they come in peace then there is no reason to press the issue. Drop your hand like the rest of us. You may be the fastest man I've ever met, but that don't make you half the man William is."

"Foreman," William said. "What's your name? I'd like to know what to tell people when they ask who I dumped in the river this time."

"My name is Foster Grant. We took this herd up from Texas to Dodge then to St. Louis. Now we're headed back to home and just trying to sell off the stragglers on our way. We aren't looking for trouble mister."

"I am," Pike said with a tone that sounded like he was taunting us. "Matter of fact I just don't think either of you are fast enough to kill Snake Pike."

Now I will admit, I had heard of Snake Pike. His name wasn't spoken in the same circles as the big outlaws or lawmen, but his name did spell trouble. He was a hired gun out of Texas that no doubt was hired on this drive for protection against anyone that wanted to threaten the job at hand. He obviously at this moment wanted to test his lore against that of William's. Not a good idea. William had never taken his guns off Foster Grant, the foreman. He knew as well as I did that as long as he had a bead on the boss, most men would fall in line. All men actually, other than a hired gun that felt like he had something to prove, like Snake Pike.

The gun from Pike's holster sprang out so fast, and hit the ground in pieces, that everyone, even me and William, were surprised. Not many men in the West still had buffalo guns, but Frank did.

His voice echoed in the hills down to the camp, "Now you don't have to worry about dropping your weapon. I dropped it for you Pike. Now you can fall in line with the rest of the men. You wouldn't have been fast enough to beat Joshua, just so you know. William taught him to use his guns and he has had years of practice since."

"I guess now we won't know, you coward," Pike yelled at the hills. "Now we won't know!"

"I do know," Frank Mathias yelled from his hidden spot amongst the rocks. "I saved you the trouble of finding out. If you care to call me a coward again, I don't mind putting the next one between your eyes. I don't mind at all Snake. You just stand there without a gun and listen to your boss, Mr. Grant, and let the boys explain why they came out here in the first place."

William was the first to speak. "I was out on a ride to find a man I been hunting for a while. Whether or not I found him is my business and his. Once Joshua showed up, everything changed. Now I'm here to save my brother, who told you he was coming to greet you, and you all took it wrong. If Mr. Grant doesn't mind, I think Joshua and I will just ride back to town. Seems Foster has some sense and the rest of you, other than you Snake, have the same mindset."

Snake Pike looked William dead in the eyes and said, "If it's the last thing I do, I'll throw dirt on you and your brother. Now that I know who you are, I'll prove to everyone in the West that I'm more a man than William Mack ever was or will be."

"Maybe you will, maybe you won't." I said it dryly. I wasn't trying to rile the boys up again. So far they had all stayed very calm, just like their boss. I really don't think they understood the type of man they were riding with in Pike. He was a bad man. Most of these boys weren't bad at all. They were just a bunch of cowboys trying to make some money while the weather was good. No cowboy wanted to be pushing cattle during the winter.

"I will get my chance Mack," it almost sounded as if he was speaking to both of us.

William spoke, "I can't wait Pike, I can't wait. I didn't ride out here looking for trouble, and it seems that's good because you don't appear to be any trouble at all, unless we count that big mouth of yours."

Pike didn't like William's words at all. I guess the comment about his big mouth was all it took to shut it for the time being because he was speechless.

"You boys gonna be okay down there," Frank asked from the cover he had. "If so, I'll see you in town."

39

We both waved at Frank as Foster Grant spoke up. "Pike," he yelled across the group of men that couldn't really believe what they had just witnessed, "if you have something to prove, that's your problem. As far as I'm concerned, these boys are fine by me. Seems to me that William is a man that means what he says. From every story I've heard he never murdered anyone. He may have killed a few men in his day, and have an odd way of disposing of them, but he seems straight forward to me. That being said, I know we have had a lot of trouble from sheriffs of towns that feel as if they have something prove. This sheriff, Mr. Joshua Mack, truly seems as though he came to say hello and just let us know this is his town. Well, it is his town. Wish I had a sheriff like that where we came from."

Just then I decided it was my turn to speak. "Mr. Grant, I appreciate the kind words and take what you said as a compliment. As far as your herd is concerned, you are more than welcome to sell your cattle in our town. Just keep a rein on Pike there. He seems to be the only man among you that feels he has something to prove. I will promise all of you now," I spoke as if I had an army at my back, which William and Frank were apt to make a man feel, "If there is any trouble out of any man jack of you, I personally will see fit to put each and every one of you in jail. If you resist that, I'm sure William has a suggestion that I wouldn't have a problem with. I don't like digging holes any more than William does."

CHAPTER VI

I climbed aboard the black and we rode south back towards town. It was not the meeting I had hoped for and I wasn't sure if William got any news as to the man he was hunting. Nearly two miles from the herd I said as much.

"William, did you pick up a trail back there?" I knew it wasn't like the West to ask a man about his business, but that was almost my hide back in that camp. I needed some answers and now that the cowboys in that group knew we were brothers, things could get a little harder.

"Dammit Joshua," William pulled up and looked right at me when he spoke. "I told you this was my affair and I didn't want to get you involved. The man I want is with that herd. I saw the tracks and the horse that made them. You see, this man for five years has had four horses, but he always has them shod the same. It's a kind of signature he's got. The shoes he always puts on his stock are marked with a six on one side and a gun on the other. Everything the man does spells trouble and he seems to be one tough man. His only downfall is he wants the whole world to know it."

"Do you think it's Pike?"

"I got that feeling when he threatened us, but if I'd known for sure I'd have killed him where he stood. The man that disgraced Maggie before killing her will die by my gun."

"How long do you think it'll be before word gets to town that we're blood, William?"

"Won't take long little brother. There's no use in trying to hide the fact now. I'm truly sorry for bringing this trouble to your town. I'm also sorry that it has to end here."

I told William words I'd been saving for a long time. "William, I have always admired you, and I need to thank you for teaching me the things I needed to learn about this rough world after Pa died. I don't think any bad man stands a chance against you and if need be, if he has help, I am sure you know that me and Frank are gonna be right by your side."

As I was speaking, Frank came from behind a large oak on the edge of the trail.

"Boys," he said in his big voice, "If Snake Pike is the man William is looking for, we got a mess of trouble coming."

I asked Frank, "You know this Pike?"

"He is a bad character but that's not the worst of it. Foster Grant is a decent enough man. He's been running cows out of the brush down in Texas for years. All the big outfits grabbed up the contracts from the army and the buyers from back East. His idea to push cattle around to the towns and sell them as he goes has worked for him. He has always had a good group of young cowboys that think the world of him and listen to what he says. The problem is, his last gun hand decided to kill a man one night in Dodge City. Turns out he didn't get away with it and hung for it. That's when Foster hired Pike. Snake Pike has been regarded as a bad man with a gun for a long time down south in Texas. They say he's killed more men than most of the known names."

"Well Frank," William said, "Do you think he's capable of killing a man in cold blood and taking advantage of a woman before also killing her?"

Frank was building a smoke as he replied, "I think that man is capable of anything that involves a gun. If I hadn't shot his piece from his holster, he'd of pulled iron on one of you for sure. I watched him in the streets of Fort Worth one time. He's fast. He just doesn't realize that he ain't the fastest. What you did last night William, was perhaps the second best shooting I ever saw."

"What's the best then?" I was just curious because when I saw William kill that man in the saloon, it was almighty fast.

"The best piece of action I have ever seen when it comes to shooting, Joshua, was the time I watched you take out the Sloan bunch. I knew you had it in you, being taught by William and all the practice you put in for years after that."

"That may have been more luck than anything, Uncle Frank."

"Luck hell," Frank almost yelled at me like when we were kids, "You're just that good."

"Well I guess little brother is all grown up," William said with a smile. "If you know that Joshua and I are better than Pike, and you don't figure on Grant and the rest of that bunch joining in, what kind of trouble are we looking at?"

Frank took a deep drag from the smoke he'd built and shifted his weight in the saddle. It seemed like an eternity before he spoke and William and I were both wondering what it was he was going to tell us.

"Pike is definitely a snake. He came by that name honest. He is very fast and tough but he ain't the problem. The real trouble is that Pike has a group of outlaws himself. He gets an honest job with a man like Grant so most folks never suspect him of being crooked. He does his fair share of the work and uses his gun when he has to. Meanwhile, he checks out the towns they pass through and gives the information to his boys, who aren't far behind him at any given time. When Pike pulls out with Grant and the herd, a few days later, Pike's men ride into town and take what they want."

I looked at Frank and then to William and asked, "How many men does he have and how do you know all this?"

"Remember my old friend that came through a month ago?"

"You mean that salty fellow that you introduced me to at dinner that night?"

"He's the one. You see, Joshua, Charlie is not just an old friend of mine, he's a Federal Marshall. He has been on the trail of Pike's outfit for quite some time. He finally put it all together a few months ago and came to see me about it. He knows how dangerous this operation is and wanted to give me some idea about what appeared to be headed to Dalston. I assured him that you could handle any trouble that came. When William got here, and I knew he was hunting a man for a while, I just figured that Pike was the man. As far as how many men he has, that is yet to be known. Charlie says that some towns are hit by five men, but he also heard a few towns were overrun by as many as ten. If ten men that

45

would ride for Snake Pike are headed this way, we got trouble coming."

"What does Charlie figure to do about it Frank?" William asked knowing that if Pike was the man he was hunting, Charlie could come in and pick up the pieces after he was finished with Pike.

"Well, William, Charlie was sent in to gather information on everything that's going on. Once he gets it all nailed on Pike, he'll show up somewhere sometime with a large group of marshals and take it all down. The problem is, with the movement, it is hard to get a group in the right place at the right time. Just last month, a group of marshals rode into a town to take down Pike's gang and were ambushed and three men died. Charlie is up against the wall with this one."

I spoke up at that moment. "I can tell you now Frank, if Pike is responsible for Maggie and Tom's death, William and I will handle him and his whole damn gang. Nobody kills one of ours and rides back through my town without paying for his sins."

"I appreciate that Joshua," William said. "I never intended to bring trouble to my little brother. I just want to get my man and not have to carry this damn name around with me the rest of my life. It's not easy being hunted by every man trying to make a name."

Frank turned his horse toward town as he looked back and put in one last bit. "It won't be easy boys, but you know damn well I got your side on this."

CHAPTER VII

Back in town, it was business as usual. The town had no idea what had happened at that herd and so far, they had no clue William and I were related. Nor did they know that Frank was our uncle. It wasn't some dark secret I wanted to hide. I just figured the longer William could conduct his hunt without the town knowing, the longer we had a card up our sleeve. We weren't sure yet that Pike was our man. Until we knew which horse he rode and could match the track with what William was following, we wouldn't know. That being the case, the town not knowing we were kin was a good thing. Add to all of that the fact that not everyone was comfortable having a man like William in our town and it wasn't going to make things any easier once they all found out. We were definitely dealing in tricky business now.

Ms. Kitchen was at her store folding a shipment of new shirts and placing them on the shelves. The door swung open and she looked up to see a very broad-shouldered man that seemed to be taller than most. She immediately felt uncomfortable. She hadn't felt this way since arriving in Dalston. Knowing that King Louis and I were watching over her, not to mention Frank stopped in daily to say hello, if not purchase something, gave her a sense of safety she had not felt since her father was alive. Ms. Kitchen spoke to the customer as she did all her customers. "Hello sir. Can I help you find anything?"

He responded in a deep voice, "Who owns this place?"

"Do you mean the building, or the store that occupies it?" she couldn't help but think that man had the meanest eyes she had ever seen.

"I mean this store. Don't catch yourself questioning me too often. I don't like being questioned. I don't care who owns this building. I want to know who operates a store without a single gun or box of ammunition on the wall. If a man can't buy bullets in the same place he buys a shirt, or piece of candy, then he has to go to two places for what he needs. That just don't seem right to me."

Ms. Kitchen thought for a second before answering the man. She wasn't sure if maybe he was just a surly man or if perhaps he truly meant her harm. "I do not like guns, sir. I understand why they are needed but I will leave the sale of such things to others. I seem to do good enough business selling household goods, cloth, clothes and candy. My store is my store and I don't feel the need to answer to you either, sir." She wasn't sure if she should have said that last part but by God, she had done fine for herself and never been talked to this way.

"You listen here little girl," he stepped closer as he said it. "You will never speak to me that way..."

Just then the man realized that he and the girl weren't alone. Someone had stepped in so quietly that he hadn't heard.

"Maybe you speak to women that way where you're from mister, but you damn sure won't do it on my watch in my town." King Louis had no reason to be cautious. It seems a man holding a double barrel has no reason to be afraid. When the man turned to see Louis pointing that shotgun at him, he froze. It's hard to miss at that range with a scattergun.

"This ain't got nothing to do with you," the man said.

"What's your name, mister?" King Louis said roughly. "I always liked to know who I was killing and I never seen you before."

The man straightened up quickly as if at attention to a commanding officer. A double barrel has that very effect on a man. All of a sudden, all the fight was out of that man.

"The name is Gentry," he said holding his hand far away from his gun.

"Well, Gentry, I'm not sure what your problem with Ms. Kitchen is, but acting the way you are don't sit well with me. Matter of fact, she may as well be a daughter to me. I don't take to anyone treating family of mine roughly."

Gentry replied, "If you didn't have that gun old man, things would work out different. That I promise."

Before Gentry could even fully get his words out, King Louis dropped his shotgun and reached out to grab the big man. He had him by the collar and had pulled the man's gun from his holster and tossed it to Ms. Kitchen. "I know you don't like weapons, but I don't want this boy, Gentry, to get any ideas about dying today."

By the time that Gentry realized he was being attacked, he reached for his weapon; of course it wasn't there. Louis had already brought his massive hand to meet the man's face. The hit was worse than anything Gentry had ever felt. His knees buckled as Louis dragged the man toward the door. Louis was as calm as he had ever been. It was almost as if he was born for a fight. He looked at Ms. Kitchen and just as calmly as if they were talking any other time, he said, "I'm going to take this outside so not to make a mess in your store, ma'am"

King Louis dragged the man out the front door of the store and across the boardwalk to the street. There were horses at the hitching rail and ladies walking about town. Every animal in sight stopped what they were doing to watch the ruckus. It was as if Gentry had never been in a fist fight before in his life. Louis landed punch after punch until he finally realized that the other man had had enough. At last, King Louis let go of Gentry and the big man fell flat to his face. The entire town was amazed. Nobody could believe what they had seen from their bartender. He always seemed such a nice man. So calm.

"If you ever come back to Dalston, you will treat everyone, especially our women, with respect. If you don't, I will personally make sure you don't get a chance to be rude again. You will not leave this town. Not unless your folks show up to claim a body to bury in a family plot. Do you understand me, boy?"

"I do. I understand mister." Gentry said it like he was thoroughly whipped. Louis had seen men like this before and knew the man wasn't done, he was just done for now. There was still a sound of hatred in his voice. He knew now was not the time to make his stand.

"Good," King Louis said loudly, "Now get on your horse and don't come back."

The crowd that had gathered from the stores, the bank, and the other various buildings, looked upon the scene

51

with amazement. They had never known Louis to be any more than a quiet man that served whiskey in his saloon. Mary happened to be standing next to Ms. Kitchen. She looked at the younger lady and said, "You never have to worry as long as my Louis is around. He thinks the world of you and will protect you as he would protect me."

William, Frank and I were riding into town when we passed a man that looked as if he'd been beat by three or four men riding out. None of us knew what to say or to think. We rode up to the crowd still standing in the street, and dismounted. As if one man, we all looked to Louis and asked, "What in the world happened here?"

"Well," Louis said clearly and with a slight excitement in his voice, "It seems Mr. Gentry, the man leaving town, had some different ideas about how to treat women than I do. I dropped in to Ms. Kitchen's store to say hello and that man was threatening her. I'm sorry sheriff, but I just won't tolerate any man treating a lady poorly."

"No apology needed," I said to Louis. "I trust any decision you make. Your wife speaks very highly of you and I trust you, and her judgment." I looked to Ms. Kitchen, "Are you okay, Ms. Kitchen?"

"I am sheriff," she said with a sigh of relief. I almost wondered if she was relieved that it was all over or if it was because I was back in town.

William spoke up. He almost always spoke at the right moment and used the correct words. "Who is Gentry? Does anyone know who that man was? If you do, it would be good to let us know so we can understand why he would attack a storekeeper."

Not a soul spoke. Not a single person knew how to address William. How do you speak to a legend? How do you not wind up in the river? How do you not upset the biggest legend this town and half of the West, has ever known? All were questions weighing on the minds of the townspeople. It felt as if I could almost read the minds of everyone. Finally I broke the silence of the crowd with some words of my own.

"People, what I'm about to say may surprise you. I support William. He is a good man. Maybe you think he is just a story passed down through the years. He is that. He is also one of the most honest and trustworthy men I've ever met."

A voice spoke from the back of the crowd. "Just last night that man threw a dead body into the Mississippi. We were all familiar with the stories sheriff, but now he's here. It's not an easy thing to accept."

Every person in town had a respect for Frank, so when he spoke, they listened. "If William wasn't faster than that young man last night, or hadn't thrown him in the river, we'd be digging a hole today. If you have a problem with the way William operates, feel free to dig the next hole. I will tell you all, whatever William does, or Joshua for that matter, I will be by their side. Now maybe you aren't aware of the trouble that is coming our way, but these two men are the ones we need, to protect us. We should all support whatever decisions they make. William is from here. He was one of us before most of you ever came along. He is, as Joshua said, a good man. Just so happens he's one of the fastest I've ever seen with a gun too."

The same man in the back spoke again, "What trouble is coming?"

As sheriff, the entire group looked to me to answer. I had hoped it wouldn't come to this. "Listen. William may never have returned to Dalston had he not been hunting a man. You all remember Tom and Maggie. They were murdered on their way west. William has been following the man responsible for quite some time. He trailed them to here. We haven't been able to determine for sure who the man is but we know he is with that herd outside of town. There is also a man with that herd, who may or may not be the one William is hunting. He is the leader of a gang that has wrecked many a small town. If they come into town, and they will, just go about business as usual. If there is any trouble, we hope to handle it without any harm to any of you."

"We trust you sheriff. If you have Frank and William by your side, then we support them too. You have always taken good care of this town and we stand by you and your decisions." King Louis spoke the words loud and proud so that everyone could hear them. I always knew if trouble came, he would be there for me.

"Thank you Louis," I replied. The townspeople were all so very quiet. There was a sense they didn't know what to think, but if Louis was with us, then they felt they should be. It was good to know that we had the support of King Louis and the town. Now we had a responsibility. It was our job to find William's man and to protect Dalston from the bad things to come. It was not a task we took lightly. Though he'd been gone for a long time, William knew the importance of this town to me. We decided to have a bite to eat with Louis and Frank to talk about a plan. It wasn't as if we could plan every detail, but we could make basic preparations and make sure we were all on the same page as far as protecting the town and stopping the man that William was looking for. I knew deep down that William had no intention of this ending in the town he had left years before.

The four of us men walked into the café and sat at a table in the far corner where there was one awkward moment that we had to decide which of us would sit with our back to the door. Seems a man that has had trouble in his life, stops to think of everything. William finally sat comfortably with his back squarely to the door. That motion in itself, said a world of words to the other men. We knew immediately that William trusted us. He knew deep inside that if any man came through the door looking for him, or any trouble at all, we were on his side. He was a very calm man.

"Listen," William said, "Before we discuss anything else, I should apologize for bringing my troubles to you."

"Nonsense!" Frank said it and he meant it. "Don't get me wrong, I have full faith in your brother. He is a true lawman and has always taken good care of our little town."

"Brother?" Louis appeared confused.

"Let me explain," Frank replied not knowing how Louis would take it. "The boys' father, my brother, was murdered when they were young. William, being a year older than Joshua, took it upon himself to find the man that killed his father and send him to his grave. The only problem was, William, after digging his father's grave, vowed to never dig a hole for any man that didn't deserve one. I swear I watched these two boys dig four or five hours straight. They loved their father and he loved them."

"So you Joshua, are the brother of the biggest legend in this part of the West?" Louis was no longer confused, but he appeared to be rather surprised.

I told him, "Yes, Louis. I am glad to have my brother here with me if trouble is headed our way. As far as you bringing us problems, William, it seems there is a gang headed our way that would have come whether or not your man had come here. Snake Pike may or may not be the man you are looking for. Until we can find the man that rides that horse, and place him on it, we won't know. We do know that Pike is bad and he has some men following his lead."

William looked up as the waitress approached. It was as if he could feel her coming up behind him. William may not have been born to kill, but he was good at watching his own back. He had in fact, over the years of men testing him, become as good as any other man with his senses and killing. He had perfected a calmness that Pa had always talked about.

"Just bring us four plates of whatever the cook has made," William said gently to her. The moment lasted for a while. She was an attractive young lady of about twenty-one. Her name was Mira and she had been in town for seven years. Her mother and father lived on a small farm on the edge of town. They didn't have much, but they did fine.

When Dee, the owner of the diner, hired Mira, the family took it as a blessing and started selling their fresh eggs and vegetables to her. It all seemed to work out. Mira made a little more for the family and the family got a new customer in their daughter's employer. William was caught up in those beautiful blue eyes she had. I'm sure in his travels he'd seen pretty eyes before. Maybe he'd never felt the job was his to protect those pretty eyes from harm.

"Yes sir," she replied. "I will keep the coffee coming too. You men look as if you have business to tend to."

As she walked away, William looked at me and said, "Who is she?"

"Her name is Mira. She's the daughter of a nice farming family we have here in town. She is a sweet girl and perhaps the reason that most people eat here," Frank said. He knew there was a connection between the two of them. At twenty-one, Mira was considered an old maid to not be married. She had had plenty of offers but none that interested her.

"She is about the prettiest thing I've ever seen," William replied. "She'll make somebody a good wife someday." We all knew he hoped it would be him.

I moved the conversation in a different direction. King Louis needed to get a meal in him and get the facts before he had to go to work at the saloon.

"Gentlemen, we have a few problems to deal with. I am glad to be able to say that I have the three of you at my side. It is my job as sheriff to defend this town against any trouble that may arise. I will do my best, as I always have.

The fact that I have you all with me has taken a little of the pressure off of me. I can't think of a better group of men to face up to trouble with."

King Louis offered up his bit of thought, "Joshua, I ran away from trouble when I brought the missus here from up north. There is no doubt that when that crooked marshal came to St. Louis, I could have handled him. I was done fighting at the time. I loaded up my supplies and my wife, Mary, and headed south. It wasn't worth the trouble. Well, I'm done running and Mary and I are very happy here. I'm not running anymore. You can count on me when you need me, all of you."

Frank took the opportunity to add his side of things. "Louis, I always felt you had it in you. These two boys have been my life since their father was murdered. I made a promise to him to take care of them. That is a promise I will take to the grave with me defending."

"I appreciate both of you," I said, feeling it was my turn to talk. I truly never thought it would come to this.

William finally spoke up. He had a harshness and seriousness in his tone that let us all know he meant business. "Look, I came here hunting what I thought to be one man. I never knew before I left that a good man by the name of Louis would ride into town to help Joshua and Frank look over things. Hell, I never thought in my wildest dreams, that my little brother would beat out the Sloan boys and be the sheriff of Dalston. I believe it is well known that I left this town because I shot a bad man and it was expected that I was a bad man. I didn't want the name or the trouble. I have thrown plenty of men in the river. None of those men left me any choice. I didn't ask for the name or the trouble, and that followed, but I guess I can say I earned it. That being said, there's plenty of room in the Mississippi. I have ro problem taking care of one last problem, but then I'm done."

We had our dinner of beef, beans and potatoes. We ate well for four men with so much on our minds. William exchanged plenty of looks with Mira throughout our meal. When we were done, and had discussed all the problems we had and the options we had, we all got up and headed toward the door. A voice spoke up from behind a newspaper in the corner. "Frank, I can't get any help here for weeks. I wish you boys the best." I recognized the voice as Charlie's. We found out later on that the Federal Marshalls had all but given up on Charlie. We were on our own. Frank later found out that Charlie was with us and gave us full cocperation from his office, but we would receive no more help from the Feds.

CHAPTER VIII

William had mentioned to me upon leaving the diner that he was going to my place to rest a while. Frank was going about his normal business, whatever that may have been. King Louis was headed home to Mary to see her a bit before he had to go to the saloon. I went my own way with my duties as the sheriff of Dalston. I went to the post office to see if perhaps there was any mail for me. A letter had come from St. Louis. It was from the sheriff of the city. He told me in the letter that his city was not affected by the gang, but a few smaller towns just north and west of him were. He cited three different small towns, about the size of Dalston, that had been raided by the gang, and he had every thought they were headed my direction. This was not big news to me but merely a confirmation. I now knew that it was all true. We must prepare for the gang. My town would not be the next victim.

When I left the post office, I continued my rounds around town that would eventually end at the saloon. This was my normal routine and I wasn't about to break out of the norm for any trouble. I stopped on the boardwalk in front of Ms. Kitchen's store just as she was closing up and locking the front door. My Lord was she gorgeous.

"Ms. Kitchen," I said nervously, "How are you this evening?"

"I am fine sheriff. Thank you for asking. I really hope you and the other men of the town can handle the trouble that is headed our way. I have always had my utmost faith in you. You helped me, Joshua, when no one else was there for me. I am now doing well in this town and I am living up to fulfilling my father's dream. All he wanted was a store in the

West. I now have a store here in Dalston. I have you to thank for that."

"We will do our best to protect you and the rest of the town, Ms. Kitchen. I am glad to know that William is here and King Louis is on our side."

"What about old Frank," she asked. "What's the story behind him?"

"Well," I said. "Frank may be the best and the worst man of us. You see, Uncle Frank fought in the war. He was a rough man according to the stories my father told me. He is very dangerous. The fact that he is family is a good thing to know. He's watched over me for years and would have done the same for William if he could've been in two places at once. He is a good man to have on your side in a fight."

"Joshua," Ms. Kitchen said, "I truly trust you. You are a kind, strong man. You are a lot like my father. I believe the two of you would have gotten along wonderfully. It means the world to me for you to help me realize my father's dream. Thank you, Joshua."

"Thank me when this trouble is behind us," I said. I tried to speak with confidence but it is a difficult thing for a man to be sure he will prevail. Doubt is an evil beast that Pa had taught me would be hard to overcome in life. I miss him so much right now. If he were here, he'd be in the thick of this with all of us.

At that, I walked Ms. Kitchen home. It wasn't dark yet but I had made it a habit to walk her home most days. Just like every other day, there wasn't much conversation between the two of us on our walk. I may never know if she enjoyed the quiet little walks as much as I did. There is something to be said for moments when nothing needs to be said.

Ms. Kitchen was safe at home, Frank was wherever Frank went and I well knew that William was resting but would join me at the saloon that evening. I went by the sheriff's office before going to the saloon. I had a stash of dried foods there and had a bite to eat. On a sheriff's salary, I could've eaten at the diner every night, but I liked putting some money aside and living rather cheap. The money I put aside was in the bank, growing and waiting for me to buy my piece of land and raise some cattle, a dream I always had. I would buy some land, pass the sheriff job to someone else, and settle down to be a rancher. Pa would have loved my plans. He never wanted much. He just wanted us kids to live a long life and have a place to call our own. I wasn't real sure, with the trouble coming, that William or I would ever have that.

There were a few letters sitting on my desk at the office. You see, in those days, I left the door to the sheriff's office open for the town's people to leave their concerns on my desk. The only time I ever locked the door when I left was at night or if there happened to be a prisoner in a cell. I hadn't had a prisoner in a few months. There wasn't much trouble in Dalston on a regular basis. Generally, the only people I had in a cell was a passer-by that had too much to drink that night and I let him sleep it off so he had no trouble to look forward to but a headache. These men would usually thank me in the morning.

I took a while to read the letters I had found on my desk. There were three of them. The first letter I picked up was from Mary. She wrote: *Dear Joshua, my Louis is very fond of you. I apologize for never having told you before about our past. He is a very good man. Louis will be by your side no matter what*

I already had the feeling that Louis was by my side and I was very thankful to have him there. The fact that his wife felt the need to tell me was fine and good.

The second letter was from Charlie, the Federal Marshall. It was as follows: *Joshua, my information tells me that the trouble you are expecting, is in fact headed your way. I wish like Hell I could get Marshalls here in time to handle this, but I can't. Seems it's you , me , and whatever help you have. Your brother, William, is a very dangerous man. He may be the best I've ever seen with a gun. I was placed on assignment to follow him a few years back. I watched him kill man after man, never a murder, and give their personal things to the local law and dump the body in the river. I never understood this until Frank explained it to me. I found no bad in the man and reported as such to my superiors. I will be there for you when you need me.*

This letter also came as a relief for me. To know that I had King Louis and the Federal Marshall by my side, along with my uncle Frank and William, was a very good feeling. I felt at that moment that no matter what happened, we could handle it.

The third letter on my desk, which was the only letter in an envelope, was very odd to me. It was from someone unknown. It read as follows: *Sheriff, I will be there when you need me. I do not have a picture perfect past but you can trust me. I know that you are the brother of the great William*

65

Mack. He happens to be my hero. He may have a few people that doubt him but I never have. I have followed him for thirteen years. I will be at yours and his side when the time comes, I swear this to you.

The letter was not signed, nor did it give any indication of the person that had written it. I was at a cross road. Did I need to watch my back more closely or could I be relieved? I wasn't sure. All I knew was I had the local Fed in town and Louis at my side. I assumed the letter was from a man that meant everything he had written. I hoped the man was going to help us. I needed the help.

I put the letters away in my top drawer, and went on about my night. After a cup of coffee and a cigar, I blew out the lamp in the little jail and walked out into the night to head to the saloon. It seemed in those days, the saloon was the place to catch up on the local business and perhaps learn where everything stood in my small town.

The night was cool and rather calm. Some nights there may be a few people just closing up shop or the sound of the blacksmith catching up on some work. Tonight was not one of those nights. The quiet was broken by the thunder of gunfire. I heard the shot before I realized it was aimed for me. The step from the boardwalk to the street saved my life. The bullet placed itself in the wall above my head. There is no feeling in the world like being shot at, other than knowing the shot missed and it is time to survive. I dove behind the corner of the building and tried to figure where that shot came from. The street was still and I saw no movement until Frank and Louis, followed by a small crowd, came pouring out of the saloon. At almost the same instant, I heard a horse in the alley across the street. Only a fool runs through the night after a man that just took a shot at him.

William was the first to speak. He said, "I guess we got that to look forward to until this is over."

"Thank God for that step or you might have been putting me in the ground," I replied. "I guess with the crowd, whoever that was, didn't think it smart to attempt another shot."

The small mob returned to the saloon with Louis. William walked with me across the dark to the alley where the gunman had been. There were fresh tracks and they were marked with a six on one side and a gun on the other. The rider had gone straight up the alley behind the buildings, so trying to see which direction the man rode was useless. We weren't about to chase anybody in the dark anyway.

"Looks like that man got shook by the odds of facing the two of us and decided to try and even the odds," William said with anger in his voice. "I never thought I was dealing with a back-shooter. There's few things in life I despise more than a coward that won't face you man to man."

"You should've known he wasn't much of a man when you found Maggie the way you did, William. Any man that would do that, will do this."

William faced me with the light of the moon shining on the rigid features of his face. I can't remember seeing that look in his eyes since Pa was killed. He finally let the words out.

"Damnit, Joshua! I don't care if there's a hundred of 'em! Bodies will float the river before I'm through. All of them and any man that claims to be a part of that group will die. If I knew for sure it was Pike, I'd ride out to that herd tonight and put six pieces of lead in him. I need to tell you little brother, I'm sorry I been gone so long. I wanted you to have a life without having to answer for your brother. It has been a long time coming, getting all this hatred out of me. When this is done, if we are still standing, I would like it if I could stick around and live out my years with the only family I got left."

I don't know if I was more shaken by the anger he showed, or the kind words he spoke. I finally choked back my shock and told him, "William, I want nothing more than to have my brother back in town with me."

It was as if William changed in a single moment. He turned and said over his shoulder, walking away, "Let's go have a drink little brother, it'll calm your nerves." He was almost immediately back to his normal, calm self. We crossed the street to the saloon and you could have heard my watch tick when we walked in. Every head was turned toward us with searching eyes, as if we had something to tell them.

"A drink on the house everybody!" Louis announced. Everybody cheered and went back to their games and drinking.

William and I moved to the bar and let Louis know we had found tracks that matched the ones of the man William had been tracking. Louis was not surprised by that at all. We sat and did our best at enjoying a beer before we decided to go to the table where Uncle Frank was sitting.

As we both turned to go to Frank's table, a man entered the saloon through the double doors. He looked very rough and like he could take care of business if it came to it. I glanced at William to try and see what he thought of this newcomer. No expression showed on William's face. He simply looked at the man and turned his head back to Frank. The two of us, William and I, went to the table and sat with our uncle. The stranger went straight to the bar to get a drink from King Louis. I had to notice such things. It's my job. William and Frank acted as if nobody else was around and started talking about the events that had occurred.

"I wish I knew the man you were hunting, William," Frank said.

"I wish I knew for a fact myself, Frank. If I did, I would handle things tonight and be done with all this trouble." William said it like he meant it and I believe he did. I knew William didn't intend to bring his trouble back home, to us. If there was any way he could have handled it before he got to Dalston, he would have. As a sheriff, I'm afraid of what trouble is to come to my town, but as a brother, I'm glad to have him with me now. Lord knows I can use the help and the trouble may have come my way whether William did or not. May as well have the fastest man with a gun I know here with me.

"I know we'll figure it all out and keep this town safe," Frank said. "I'm glad you are here William. Joshua and I have never had trouble like this come our way. The Sloans were a bad bunch but not like this. It seems as if we are in a bind until we know who the leader is and can figure the odds we are facing. There is no feeling like not knowing how many men you are facing and who they are."

I finally spoke up, "Did y'all see the man that just walked in?" I was not sure if the two of them were aware anybody had entered the bar. They both shot me a look like I was almost wrong for even asking.

"Yeah, I seen that gent before," William said.

"Me too. I can't remember when or where but I know that ragged face. He sure looks to be a tough one," Frank added.

"Well, I don't guess I've ever seen him but then again he probably ain't never been to Dalston before. You two both know I'm not well traveled. He does appear to be one tough man. I sure hope this don't amount to more trouble for you or me, William."

" That man isn't trouble, Joshua. I just remembered where I saw him before. He is fast with a gun but not a bad man at all. He happens to be an acquaintance of my pal, Charlie. I met him in St. Louis when I went up one time. I watched him walk all over that town. He is not a man to mess with. Charlie says he is one of the hardest men he has ever met. I am not sure if Charlie sent him here or he's just passing through." Frank said all of this like he was telling us a story and William and I were still kids.

William added, "That's where I know him from. I have spent plenty of time in St. Louis. I remember him. I watched him whip a man one day for talking wrong to a lady."

"Well, I will take a good man on our side any day, if that's what he is. I can use all the help I can get."

"I'm not sure he is here to help, Joshua," Frank said dryly. "I am not sure what he would be here for."

"I hope it's to help us," William spoke. "Otherwise he can die like the rest of them."

"William, I think this is a little more personal to you than it is to us."

"You're damned right it is, Frank. I was the one that found Tom and Maggie, not you. Do you know what it feels like to give up the woman you love to a man that you think can give her a better life just to find them both dead in another state?"

"I don't know what that feels like, William, but I do know that your father told me years ago to take care of you and Joshua. I have been given a duty and I will be honest right now, it was easier to keep an eye on Joshua than it was to watch over you. He stayed here in Dalston and you didn't"

"Look, men, I am well aware that I don't have to worry about you," I said to break up the conversation. "However, I have a duty to protect this town."

As we were speaking, the big man had gotten his beer and turned to take in the scene. He had the look of a man that noticed every little detail. As if we had all three called him over, he walked straight up to our table in the corner. He was big. The gun on his side was worn low and well kept. Before I could even stand and introduce myself, he spoke.

"Joshua Mack, did you get my letter?"

It took a moment before it occurred to me. This had to be the man that left the unsigned letter on my desk. I finally responded. "Yes, I got your letter. Care to join us?" I asked.

Just when that large man was about to speak and it appeared he may join us, he was hit from behind with a bottle. The three of us had no way of warning him because he was right up against our table and his huge body blocked the view of the rest of the room. When the bottle hit his head, it shattered but he didn't so much as wince. He just calmly looked at us and said, "Excuse me gentlemen, I'll only be a minute and then we can talk."

The big man spun to look right into the wrong end of a gun. As if he'd been in this position a hundred times before, he immediately grabbed the barrel of the gun and pulled it from the small stranger's hands. This stranger at that point had a look of fear in his eyes and the big man tried his best with one punch to take that look away. The smaller man had no chance. He fell to the floor and was trying to crawl to the door. The big man grabbed him up off the floor with one hand by the back of his shirt. Then he spoke. "This is one hell of a way to get to know each other. Do you care to tell me what all this is about or should I just finish the job?"

The frightened stranger, looking as if he'd rather be anywhere but right there right then, responded, "I was paid to do it."

"Who paid you? Was it worth it?"

"I don't know his name. He met me out on the trail and described a large man that would be coming to town and

I was to get you out of the picture. I thought maybe the bottle would do it and you'd just be laid up for a while. I never shot nobody before. I'm real sorry mister."

The big man had just placed the man back on his feet and let him stand on his own. He spoke real loud as if hoping the whole town would hear. "I'm gonna let you leave town now. If I ever see your face again I'll kill you. Sheriff, do you have a problem with that?"

"I have no problem at all. Matter of fact, I'd like nothing more than to keep men like this out of my town," I said. "If on your way out of town, you see the man that paid you, tell him that he's got more trouble than he thought coming. I never did take to a man that can't take care of his own business. Consider yourself a lucky man, stranger. I'd have sat right here and drank my beer, even if this fella decided to kill you with his bare hands."

At that, William stood up. He looked the big man in the eyes, and as the small stranger was heading for the door, he stuck out his hand and said, "My name is William Mack."

CHAPTER IX

"I know who you are," the big stranger said as he took William's hand to shake it. "I've been following you for years. My name is Turner. Don't know if that is my first or last name. It's always just been Turner."

William then asked, "Why have you been following me all this time?"

"You rode through a small town just north of St. Louis bout thirteen years ago. My father was all I had in this world and we didn't have much to our name. He was attacked by a mob when he got in their way of robbing the bank there. He was shot down in cold blood and he never even carried a sidearm. I watched the whole thing from our wagon. Father was going in to make a small deposit from us selling some grain to the General Store. I guess I was twelve then. Those men shot him full of holes and went to ride out of town about the time you was riding in. I remember one of them drawing a gun up on you and your gun came from nowhere and killed all three of them."

The two of them, Turner and William, made their way to a couple of chairs at the table. Once there, William continued the conversation.

"I remember that. At the time, I had no idea they had robbed the bank or killed a man. All I knew was there were a lot of men trying to kill me because of my name. When that first man drew on me, I had no choice but to protect myself."

Turner added, "It was after you had shot them that I saw you place their bodies over the saddles on their horses and ride them down to the river. The sheriff of that town, and half the town, followed you. We had all heard the stories, and now the stories were to be confirmed. When the sheriff asked you what you were doing, you looked him dead in the eyes and said, 'There's plenty of room in the Mississippi.' Everybody in attendance was shocked. The stories were one thing, but to see you kill like that in person and watch you dump those bodies in the river, was chilling."

"I'm sorry you had to see that as a kid," William said, almost sadly.

"Those men, whoever they were, had just killed my father. I was happy to see you do what you did. After that, you probably stuck around town two days before moving on. In those two days, I got father's money out of the bank, sold our three mules and bought a horse. Father had an old saddle I used and a rifle at the cabin. I then bought myself a bedroll and pistol and a little grub. When you left town, I left town behind you. I been following you ever since."

"I never knew you were there, and I've picked up plenty of folks following me over the years. How'd you do it without me ever knowing?"

Turner looked up from his beer. "I never got too close and would sometimes leave a days ride between us as long as the weather was good and I could still pick up your trail."

William was a little shocked. He finally said, "You turned into quite a man, son. I remember watching you handle yourself once in St. Louis. That man, like the one tonight, never had a chance."

"I watched you for years and learned, the best thing to be in any situation is calm. If a man keeps his head, he can handle anything. I never had any intention of meeting you face to face. I just didn't have anything left and thought following you was a good idea. I learned all I know about surviving in this world from watching you."

I spoke up, "What finally brought you to meet William, Turner?"

Turner leaned in to the table and said, "You all know that a man hears things in towns and camps that maybe he should or shouldn't know. Being that I never made contact with any of you before, men tell me things they should have kept to themselves. I was in a camp of maybe eight men, just northwest of here, having a cup of coffee one night. They obviously didn't know me and weren't worried at all about me knowing what they were talking about. The man in charge was saying that he knew for a fact that William was headed to Dalston and they could finally take care of him as they robbed the town. They were all a very tough looking crowd and talking as if they knew what they were doing. Now, being a traveled man, following William, I had heard of this gang that went from town to town taking what they wanted. I sat, drinking coffee, and listened. Just before I told them thanks for the hospitality but I needed to be moving on, the man in charge, said he couldn't wait to put William in the Mississippi."

William seemed calm. He finally asked, "Do you know who any of these men were?"

"No sir I don't. I haven't done much with my life but follow you and try to learn your every move. You did my job, avenging my father and I have the most respect for you. When those men said they were headed here, I felt the need to finally introduce myself and let you know. My father was killed in cold blood and I feel you are the only friend or family I have left. I know that sounds odd but it's true."

"That doesn't sound odd to me at all," William said. "I should've come back to my family long before now but was afraid to bring my name and the trouble that goes along with it home to Joshua and Uncle Frank. I never intended to live this life, but I damn sure didn't want to put the only family I have in danger. That being said, I am happy to be able to have a beer with my brother and uncle. I finally feel at home. I'm very sorry you don't have a home, Turner."

"I have made my home a trail behind you," Turner said quietly. "I've followed you to places I would have never seen had it not been for you. You are like a brother I never knew."

Frank finally spoke up. "Home is wherever you make it, son. My home has been here with Joshua. I'm sure I speak for the both of us when I say, it is good to have William back. We would have been glad to have followed him as well. Turner, you have seen more on the trail than we ever will."

William responded to that, "Uncle Frank, Joshua, I am glad to be back here with you. I wish it hadn't come to this, but it did. Now, it appears we got a little more help. Can we count on you, Turner?"

"You have had my help more than you think already, William. I was there in New Orleans when you faced five armed, tough men. I remember hearing you say to yourself as you threw those bodies in the river, that you had no clue how you came out of that fight. I was in the stable and had hit two of those men with my rifle. With the gunfire and the crowd, you never even realized that you had help, but you did."

"I guess I owe you, Turner," William said. "Thank you for that. I really thought I had just gotten lucky. I guess the luck was that you were there."

"You all can count on me, to the end. I have had no real family since father was killed and I would be glad to be a part of this family. I owe you more than I can ever repay."

"You don't owe me a thing, Turner, but to have you here to help , is a good thing," William said. He spoke as if he knew that things were going to be fine now.

"So, now we have William, Joshua, Turner, Charlie and me," Frank said. "Turner said there were at least eight of them. I will take eight on us five any time. Seems like all we need is to figure this whole thing out and who is involved. Once we know that, we can take care of business."

"It's been a very interesting day boys," I said. "I think I am going to go home and get some rest. William, are you staying at the house tonight?"

"No," William said as if he had something on his mind. "I'm staying out tonight. I did enjoy a nice bed last night but I can't get too comfortable. I will set up camp outside of town and keep to myself for a day or two. Thanks for the offer little brother."

William stood up from the table. The entire crowd left in the bar stared into their cups as not to have to look into the eyes of the man that had changed the little world they knew. Not one of these men wanted to upset the man they knew would be the one to save their town. He was very peaceful, William was. He just wasn't a man to cross. I believe every man in the saloon, all of them regulars, knew without William we were in for trouble. Our town hadn't had any trouble since the Sloan gang came through.

Turner, soon after William, excused himself. We had no idea where he was headed but we kind of figured him to stay close to William.

Frank looked straight into my eyes and said, "I figure we got some real trouble headed our way. I would have never worried about that with you and William around, if it were not for Turner telling us there are at least eight men. Add to that the fact that one of them has no problem shooting at you in the cover of night and somebody has no trouble paying a stranger to take out a man that has come to help us and we are in real trouble. I promised your dad that I'd do my best to take care of you and your brother. I sure wish your father was here right now. We could use a man like him right now."

"We have me, you, William, Charlie, Turner, and King Louis," I added. "What do you mean about my pa?"

Frank got real calm and quiet. It was almost as if he didn't want to speak. He finally did. "Your father was a very fast man with a gun. Where do you think you and William got it from? You see, Joshua, I didn't think I'd ever tell you or William any of this. Your Pa was one tough man. We went to war together. We weren't sure that fighting other folks from our country was a good idea, but then again I'm sure that most men in the war were that way. Once you get in battle, you either get to fighting or you die. Your father went to fighting. He was Hell on wheels in the war. Had I not stuck close to him, I may not be here today."

"He never told us about any of that, Uncle Frank. He was such a peaceful man when we were growing up."

"Joshua," Frank said coldly, "If my brother, your father, had had a weapon the day that man braced him, he'd be here today. William wouldn't have turned out the way he is and you'd probably still both have a dad. Your old man was the reason that our entire regimen came out of the war alive."

"Was he really that bad?" I wasn't very comfortable asking that question. I thought my father to be a peaceful saint.

"Your dad snuck out of camp one night. We knew we were to have a battle the next day and it was going to be bloody. He waited until we were all asleep and left on foot. Your dad went through the woods and took every horse the opposing troop had. He also, like a whisper in the night, took every rifle they had. He then led those horses back to our camp and in the morning, when we were supposed to go to battle, we discovered from our scout that those other boys had left. We were outnumbered and should have had plenty of dead to bury that day, but your dad changed that all by his lonesome. He was one hell of a fighter."

"He never told us any of that, Uncle Frank," I said.

"He wasn't one to ever talk about the war. Your father was my hero. He was one man that I looked up to. It's like you see William, as a hero."

"I do think William is a man I look up to, Uncle Frank."

Frank was silent for a second. He almost seemed as if he were done talking. Finally, he broke the quiet. "You should look up to William. He killed the man responsible for your father's death. He has a way about him that confuses most folks but that doesn't change the man he is. You and your brother would make your father proud, Joshua. We will get through this trouble and let's hope when we do, we can all settle down and live out our lives. It's what Dale would have wanted."

"Thank you, Uncle Frank, for telling me all of that. I never knew that Pa was a fighter. I am proud to know William is here. I hope when this is all over, he will settle with us. I have wanted to ask you something for a while."

"You can ask me anything, Joshua," Frank said.

"Did you help me that day with the Sloans?"

"I wanted you to think you did that on your own. I was in the top of the hostler's barn, Joshua. I had a clean shot on one of the Sloans, but before I could squeeze the trigger, you spun on a heal and shot him through the chest. I was prepared to help you. I had never seen you face three or more men before. I wanted to help, but it turns out you didn't need it. I truly believe you are as bad if not worse with a gun than William. You are fast."

"I truly appreciate the fact that you were there for me, Uncle Frank. I don't know if I'm anywhere near the gunman William is. It's good to know we are both here when trouble is headed toward our town. I should get home. It seems I'll need some rest."

At that, I stood to leave and Frank just stayed put. It never failed; Frank came and went as he pleased. We never knew what he did, but he was there when we needed him.

"Frank. Thank you for telling me those things. I do hope when this is all over, you, William and I can all live here in peace. I'll see you tomorrow."

At that, I paid Louis what we owed him and left through the double doors. I went to the big black, and started to saddle up. I was almost on my horse when I was grabbed from behind. The man doing the grabbing immediately wished he hadn't. I spun as he grabbed me and swung. My first punch missed as he ducked, but my second, a left, caught him in the mouth. Blood poured from his face and I didn't stop there. I got ahold of the man and drove my knee into his stomach. He was too busy bleeding from the mouth to defend any other attack. I soon had hit him two or three more times and had him spun around and in shackles. At this moment, I retied the big black to the hitching post and walked this man to the jail. He tried a few times to resist but being shackled has a weird effect on a man. He went. He didn't have much choice.

We arrived at the jail and I threw him in the first cell. I didn't even feel like asking him any questions. I locked the cell and went right back out the front door and headed toward my horse. I had had enough for the day and just wanted to go home and get some shuteye. I was worn out and needed sleep. I would question the man in the morning.

CHAPTER X

It had been a very long day, sunup to late after sunrise. I was exhausted. I will say, without William around the house tonight, I was cautious. I took the saddle off the black and looked around very carefully before heading in the house. Nothing seemed to be out of place and I saw no tracks in the yard other than mine and William's. I thought to myself, maybe there was a chance these fellows, being from out of town, didn't know where I lived. That didn't stop me from worrying. All in one day, I had watched a sunrise with a brother I hadn't seen in years. I rode out to greet a cow camp and was almost in a shootout. I returned to town to discover one of our local store-owners, Ms. Kitchen, had to be rescued by Louis, from a stranger that I'm not sure has any association with the trouble headed our way. I then met a man, Turner, that has followed my brother for years and I believe is an ally to us. All I wanted to do was get home and get some rest and I was attacked as I tried to get on my horse. It was a very busy day and I had too much on my mind. I just wanted to lie down and rest.

I woke in the morning to rise and head to the stove to make coffee. Before I went to bed, I filled the stove with logs so there would be heat in through the night. You see, the nights were cool, no matter how hot the days seemed to be. If a man didn't leave a fire burning he would not only wake to a cool house, he would wake to have to build a new fire for coffee. No man wanted to have to build a new fire for coffee.

I got out of bed and shook my boots and pulled them on. I strapped on my gun belt. I hadn't slept that well in a long time. I'm not sure if it was the trouble headed our way and the surprise of our two days together, William and I, or if I just needed the sleep. Either way, I woke with a clarity that didn't sit well with what I was used to. Normally, I woke from a toss and turn night, to just be tired again. It was no way to live, but it was the way I lived.

I went into the next room to put coffee on. There was already some coffee going on the stove. I just figured William had dropped for coffee. I had enjoyed his company the day before. It had been a long time since I had even seen him, much less had a cup of coffee to start a day with him. I had missed my brother for a long, long time. He was my hero since Pa had died. He had to do what he had to do and his actions separated us for years. When the coffee was done, I poured myself a cup and headed to the porch to watch the sunrise. I stepped out the door, onto the porch, and before I could take in the outdoors, I was surprised by a strange voice.

"You got trouble headed your way, sheriff," the voice said.

I reached for my pistol but, before I could get my hand to it, the man on my front porch warned me.

"If you wanna die, go ahead. If I wanted to kill you I would have shot you long before you had a chance to reach for your piece."

"Who are you and what do you want," I asked. I couldn't remember a time in my adult life that I had been caught so off guard. If this man had wanted to, he could have killed me as I stepped out of the door. There was a sudden sense of relief that the gent on my porch had mentioned trouble and had not killed me himself. This man was either not a part of the trouble or was a fair man and did not believe in cold-blooded killing. I was alive and that's all that mattered at the moment.

"I'm not an enemy, sheriff. I may not have any part in this whole thing at all. I just thought I should share some information with you. As for who I am, my name is Samuel."

"Samuel who," I responded.

"It's just Samuel, sheriff."

"Do you always surprise men on their front porch first thing in the morning?"

"No sir, I heard some news and felt the need to share it with you. You see, Mr. Mack, I was hired on at the Sterling ranch. My job there is to keep things running smooth. I don't push cattle. I don't cook. I just make sure the boys get the job done and Old Man Sterling is safe, along with his investments."

"You're a hired gun, is that right?"

"I have never used my gun unless a man forced me to. Sterling hired me to make sure business went well. He may have never told you, but the old man has a son. He's a wild card. Even Sterling himself is afraid of what might happen with him around."

"Is this the trouble you came to tell me about," I asked Samuel. "Or is there more?"

"I have not met the son yet, sheriff. All I know is that a few of the men talk about him like he is a danger to the ranch and the town. You would think they were talking about

The Kid himself. They tell stories, around the fire at night, as if he has the gun of Bonnie and the presence of Earp."

"From what you've heard, Samuel, do you think he is really a concern of mine, or is he liable to be your trouble?"

"Sheriff," he spoke like he meant it, "I would not be on your front porch, telling you anything, if I didn't think he was going to be trouble for the whole town. His father has worked hard to build the Sterling into what it is. The son has been gone for years, trying to make his own way. He didn't want to just work for his father and inherit the ranch. He, according to a few of the older hands, wanted power as soon as he could get it. I learned a long time ago, any man hunting power is dangerous."

"Will he not listen to Sterling himself?"

"That's the problem, sheriff. From what I understand from the men, he is headed our way and even the old man is worried. He, Mr. Sterling, has asked me to stay close to him and close to the main house at the ranch. There is nobody still working at the ranch that was around when he left, so no one can identify him."

I thought for a moment and replied, "I worked on the Sterling place when I was a kid. I remember that the old man had just sent his son away to attend school in the East. I was already quitting that job and had become sheriff before he was to come home."

"Well Mr. Mack, this son went away to become a lawyer." Samuel had a sudden tension about him, as if he were truly worried about what was to come. Then he added, "He got the education he needed, but he also met some very ruthless, and powerful people. The influence he was under was not exactly what we here in the West think of as honest. The way I understand, the son learned that power is the most important thing in life. He doesn't think anything like his father. Sterling worked his tail off to get what he has. You should already know that sheriff."

I thought about what was said for a bit. Then I replied, "Mr. Sterling was always very fair to me. He gave me a job when my pa died, and I truly needed it. I cut horses and pushed cows for him for a few years, before our sheriff was killed and I had to protect the town. After I took care of the Sloans, the town made me sheriff and here I am with the most trouble I have faced since they put this star on my chest."

Samuel took a sip of his coffee. I realized at that moment he had been inside my house. I must have slept heavier than ever. He finally spoke. "I heard your brother took care of the man that murdered your pa. He built quite a legend around his name. When I'm back East, the kids read his story in dime novels and run through the streets with sticks they pretending they're guns, yelling, 'There's plenty of room in the Mississippi.'"

"William never wanted that name, Samuel. He took care of the man that killed pa and a few men were threatened by him so he had them coming at him to try and prove he wasn't really that fast. The problem was, pa taught him to shoot at a young age, him being the oldest son and pa knowing if the day ever came he wasn't around, William would have to take care of me and the farm. William used to ride away from town, when he had a break from working with pa, and practice drawing his piece and aiming true. He would take me with him sometimes, and I would copy everything he did. The things he taught me are probably the only reason I've been able to wear this badge for years. When he killed the man that had killed our father, no one could believe a boy could be that fast, because that man was supposed to be real fast. William is not an evil man, he just seems to have pa's sense of right and wrong. If you're right, William will ride with you to the end, but if you're wrong, he will put you in the mighty river with the rest."

Samuel nodded then added, "I know all about William. I also know all about Louis and you. I have heard some stories about your uncle Frank and I believe he is cut from an old mold. You have the men you need at your side. I came this morning to tell you about Sterling's boy and let you know that you have our support from the ranch. You see, the way I see it, if the town is in trouble the ranch is too. If that bank gets robbed, Sterling loses money. If you need help, call on me."

"Thank you, Samuel. When you get back to the ranch, tell Mr. Sterling I'm sorry I haven't been out in a while to see him. I'm sure he understands I have been busy. Also, not many people in the town know William is my brother. We don't want people thinking I am partial in my duty. If William had ever gone to the wrong side of the law, I would like to think he would have never come back to Dalston and put me in a position to have to handle him. He returned because he is following a man that killed his first ove. That man happens to be with that herd on the edge of town."

"The boss's son could be with that herd as well. How does William know for sure his man is with them?"

91

"The man that he is hunting has changed horses many times over the five years William has been on his trail. He always shoes his horses with a six on one side and a gun on the other."

Samuel jerked his head up like he'd been shot, "Did you say a six on one side and a gun on the other?"

"Sure did. What's that mean to you?"

"That's the only fact we know about Sterling's boy. We figure, he's been gone so long, the boss himself may not even recognize him. Like you said yourself, he was gone before you hired on and hasn't been back since."

"You mean to tell me, the man William is hunting, the man I am worried about protecting the town from, and Sterling's boy, are the same person?"

"It sure appears that way, sheriff. Looks like we got big trouble heading straight for us. I need to get back to the ranch. Like I said before, if you need me, just send for me."

I took the last sip of my coffee. I then stood to shake Samuel's hand and I said, "Thank you again for the visit Samuel. I hope we all make it through this alive."

"Me too, sheriff. Take care."

At that, Samuel mounted his horse and rode away. I needed to get to town and see Mary and Ms. Kitchen. I had made it such a habit to see them every morning, if one day I wasn't there, they may get worried. Lord knows we already had enough to worry about around town without me breaking routine and worrying the women. I went inside to get my rifle and put out the fire in the stove. Then I went to the barn and saddled the black.

CHAPTER XI

95

When I arrived in town, I went straight to making my rounds. I was walking past the little storage shed behind the saloon where Mary kept the stuff she used to cook up the food Louis served. She appeared from inside.

"Good morning sheriff," she said so politely, just like every morning since they got to town. "Emily is worried to death about you. You seem to be a little late today."

"Yes ma'am, I had some surprise company at the house this morning."

"No trouble I hope. Seems we have aplenty of that coming."

" No ma'am, it was not trouble. It was a man that works for Mr. Sterling."

"He wouldn't happen to be a nice looking, well-dressed man of about forty, would he? A man like that came in yesterday for lunch and was asking a few questions about the sheriff of our town."

"That's him, Mary. He was hired by the old man to take care of his business. He has all the good hands he needs, but he hired this man to handle any trouble that may come his way. It seems that Mr. Sterling has a son that has been gone for a long time and it's believed that he has returned. That man you speak of came by my place this morning to warn me that the younger Sterling is trouble."

"Well sheriff, I have faith in you and the men that stand behind you, including my Louis. You better get over to Emily's place and say good morning before she goes looking for you. That is a beautiful young lady and she has a real catch in you."

"What do you mean by that?" I asked out of curiosity.

"Why Joshua Mack, don't tell me you don't realize she is hung up on you. That girl wants the chance to love you forever. When you finally get around to asking, she will say yes before you can even finish."

"Thank you Mary. That's some information I'm finally glad to hear. I'll head over to her right store now."

I turned and walked in the direction of the store. I had done this every morning since becoming the sheriff of Dalston. Today was different. I just received confirmation from Mary that the lady I'm in love with, and planned to spend the rest of my days with, also was in love with me. I had hoped for the longest time that that was the case, but was never certain. The only thing stopping me from courting her was the fact that I hadn't quite saved enough to buy my own spread. I didn't feel like a badge was much to offer a woman. She deserved much more than a man whose job could make her a widow at any time. It's very unnerving that I learn she wants to be with me when the worst trouble I've ever had to deal with is headed my way. That thought added a sense of importance and urgency to the situation. The sooner we figured all this out, the sooner I could become the man I need to be to ask her to be mine.

"Well Joshua Mack, where in the world have you been?" Ms. Kitchen's words were spoken with a voice of concern that I couldn't remember hearing since she came to town alone and said she wanted to set up a store.

"Ms. Kitchen, I had some unexpected company on my front porch this morning. It was important that I speak to this man. He had much news to tell me and it was very helpful with the trouble that is on its way to Dalston. I am truly sorry I am late getting to town."

"You know well that Mary and I worry about you if you are even the least bit late." She said it like she really meant it. "You had me about ready to come looking for you, Joshua."

"I said I'm sorry, Emily." I knew as the name left my mouth that I was in for trouble. I had never called her anything besides Ms. Kitchen. It must have been the excitement of knowing she was going to be my girl, if I lived through all this mess.

"What did you just call me, Joshua?" She had a smile on her pretty face when she asked.

"Ms. Kitchen, I called you Emily. I have hoped that wouldn't come out until the right time but here we are." I was speaking very nervously. I hadn't wanted anything in my life more than this lady that was standing before me so beautiful in her dress.

"Well perhaps there is truly no better time than right now. I am very aware of the trouble that is headed to Dalston, sheriff. I am also aware of the fact that you haven't been able to take your eyes off me since I first arrived in town. I never felt like a beautiful lady until I met you, and you have always treated me as such. You need to take care of your business and protect this town. When you are done, I fully expect you to be at my door calling on me. Do we understand each other Joshua?"

I was very uncomfortable. None of this needed to happen now. I had no choice though. I had to respond. I took a deep breath and said, "I will do my best to still be standing after all this is over and come to see you."

"You better be alive when this is all said and done Joshua Mack. I didn't ever want it to all come down to this, but you are the man for me and I want my man to be alive."

"I will be Ms. Kitchen."

"Don't ever call me miss again until the day you are willing to call me Mrs. Mack. My name is Emily. It won't be long before this is all over and you may address me properly as Mrs. Mack." She spoke with an intent that was very clear. This beautiful woman standing before me wanted to be my wife and all I had to do was get rid of the trouble that faced me. That's all.

"Emily, I want nothing more in life than to figure out who is behind the problem facing our town and to settle down with you afterward. Hopefully my brother William will stick around too."

"William is your brother? I thought there was some strange relation between you and him. Not many know yet, do they Joshua?"

"No ma'am. Not many people know that William is my blood. He left town a long time ago after averging our father's death. Since then, he has built a name as a very fast man with a gun. He is a good man though, regardless of the legend that follows him." I was sure hoping she, of all people, believed me when I spoke highly of William. It was hard for me not to think that some folks would judge me for having what appeared to be a ruthless bloodline. Most people in town were aware that Frank was my uncle but, old Frank was an innocent to them. An outsider with an entire legend built around him, was a different thing all together.

"I could never bring myself to doubt you, your family or your judgment Joshua. You helped me to get settled and have watched over me since the day I arrived here in Dalston. Louis has always watched over me as well, but it is more of a fatherly act with him. It is a different thing with you. I've always hoped the time would come when we could share our feelings with each other; I never imagined it would come at such a dangerous time. You go take care of your duty now sheriff and protect our town. Just don't forget you are needed alive and well when all this is over."

"Yes ma'am Emily. I will see you soon." At that, I turned and headed toward the post office to see if perhaps there was any new news for me. On my way across the street, I heard the loudest racket coming from the jail.

In my eventful morning, with Samuel coming to see me and Ms. Kitchen speaking openly to me, I had completely forgotten about the man that I had whipped the night before and thrown in jail. He was causing such a fuss that if anyone had overslept, they were surely awake now. I barely remembered the night, much less what this man looked like. I crossed the boardwalk very slowly to give him a chance to get all his yelling over with before I had to question him and find some things out.

CHAPTER XII

I arrived at the jail and opened the door. As I did, his loudness turned from the outside window toward the inner part of the building. I couldn't understand every word he was trying to say. He said something about being knocked out and whipping the man that had done it. I got a good laugh at that. He caught me from behind the night before and I had still whipped him pretty bad. What made a man think he could do something a second time that he had failed so poorly at the first time around?

"You," he yelled as I approached his cell. "I'll whip you, you'll see!"

"You should never greet a man you don't know with an insult sir. It is best to start with an introduction."

The man behind those steel bars continued to be angry and yell as I continued with my speech.

"My name is Joshua Mack. I'm the sheriff here in Dalston. What's your name son?"

I'm guessing maybe it was my calmness, and perhaps the fact that he was locked behind bars and knew if I tired of him, I could close back the door and walk on about my business, but he settled a bit. He asked me for a glass of water and as I turned to oblige, he finally spoke in a calm state of mind.

"My name is Dave Young and I work for the Sterling Ranch. Can I have that glass of water now?"

"Here's your water, Dave. You must be one of the new boys out at the ranch. I don't recall ever seeing you before. What on Earth brings you in to town to try to take me on, Dave Young?"

"I hired on about a month ago and haven't ever been to town. I was sent to attack you. The man said there'd be a twenty dollar bonus in it for me, win or lose. Obviously, that gent didn't know any more than me what kind of sheriff this town's got. As for this morning, I was just upset about getting whipped. It is clear that I'm not the man for that job. You're one tough man, sheriff." He had calmed quite a bit. I walked to the small stove in the corner to light the fire, and I put on coffee for the two of us.

"I'm gonna leave you where you are for now, but as you calm and I learn a little more throughout the day, as long as I'm convinced you are of no harm, I'll release you. If you ever try me again I'll make sure you never get a chance to fight again. I'm in no mood to have to watch my back for a greenhorn like you. I have much more to worry about than the likes of you."

He looked down at the floor, as though disappointed with himself for such a foolish act, but twenty dollars is a lot of money to not have to draw iron for. I finally heard the coffee boil and poured us each a cup. Seems coffee has a way of making a man at ease.

"Well," I said. "I know the old man didn't send you; I used to work for him. I'm really hoping this new man, Samuel, didn't either. He sure seemed mighty honest when I spoke with him this morning."

"You're right sheriff, the old man loves you. I've never heard him speak more highly of anyone. He says there'd be no Dalston and probably no Sterling Ranch left if you hadn't taken out them Sloan boys. Samuel most certainly didn't send me either. He knows what you mean to this town and to Mr. Sterling and has quite a fondness for you. It was a new man. One I met out on the edge of the range. He doesn't work for us."

"Did you by chance get a name or a description, Dave?"

"It was getting close to dusk yesterday when he rode up on me sheriff. He was a big man. Bigger than you or me. I didn't get a look at his face with it coming on to dark. Also, he wore his hat pulled down in the front as to cover his face. I'm really sorry I can't be of more help and I am sorry for taking a swing at you. I was hunting a job real bad when Mr. Sterling hired me and any extra cash in a man's pocket, with winter coming in a few months, is a big help."

"I do understand that Dave but I hope that earning money in a bad way is a lesson you never have to learn again. Did you at least see which way this man was headed when he left?"

"He made sure I rode away before he did. He seemed very careful about everything sheriff. He did say he was to meet me back in the same part of the ranch as last night, tonight, to pay me my twenty dollars and find out how my efforts turned out."

"Which part of the ranch were you on?"

"I was in the south area, down not far from the bend in the river. There's a little clearing there where the cattle like to eat."

"I know just the place. I worked for the old man for a few years before being put into the sheriff's job."

"I was hoping you would release me in time to get there to collect my pay, sheriff," Dave said. He seemed very truthful about the whole thing. He was just a young cowhand trying to earn some extra cash before winter. He couldn't have had a clue with what he was going to run into with me. I was sure hoping he had learned a little caution from the whole mess.

"I'll release you this afternoon, Dave. Please understand my need to take care of a few things before I can. I really would hate to have to whip you again, or even worse, draw iron and dig a hole for you." We were at this point speaking as two gentlemen that had not had a previous problem.

"I understand, sheriff. I just hope he shows tonight to pay up."

"He will. You can bet on that. This man really wants to know what's in store for him when he finally has to confront me. It makes for a ruthless man when he's willing to put up money to find out what he's dealing with. I will release you and I will be there with you when he comes."

Dave got a little excited when he spoke. "You don't get it. He said come alone or I would never see my twenty dollars. I could sure use that money and I earned it taking that whipping from you."

"I know that ranch as good, or better, than the old man himself, Dave. I will ride out early and he will never know I'm there. I just need to know what I am dealing with too. I have some things to tend to Dave. I will be back around noontime with some beef and beans for you."

"Thank you, sheriff. You seem like a right honest man and once again I am sorry I ever took a swing at you."

"I know that Dave. You're the one that has to wear that black eye back to the ranch and explain where you've been all day to Mr. Sterling. As long as I can trust this won't happen again, I will hold no hard feelings."

"Thank you. I'm gonna get some rest until you bring that lunch. Could I have one more cup of coffee before you go?"

I poured Dave a cup and handed it to him. I stood at the edge of the cell and watched the man drink his fill. I thought for a second, that this must be a setup. ¯hen I realized that in no point of our conversation did I doubt his word, and finally, I trusted everything this man told me. He was just a cowhand trying to make a few bucks.

CHAPTER XIII

I left the jail, and stepped out on the street. Just as my boots hit the boardwalk, I heard words from a familiar voice.

"Joshua," the voice said. "We got us a real problem."

I spun around, trying to act as if they hadn't caught me completely off-guard, and I responded, "What is it Frank?"

I could tell in William's movements and in his anxious manner that something was eating at him. I hadn't seen him look that way since he vowed to kill the man that murdered Pa.

William pushed past Frank and said urgently, "They took Mira. By the Lord Joshua, we have to get her back, and if they laid a finger on her, I will put every last one of them in the Mississippi!"

"Who took her Frank?" I asked Frank because William had blood in his eyes and was in no shape to give me facts. He was in the mindset that whoever it was needed to die, and they should die today. I knew since the day he first saw her in the café, he wanted her the way I wanted to be with Ms. Kitchen. I probably had the same look in my eyes, the look William had yesterday in the café, the first time I met Emily. There I go calling her Emily in my thoughts. I sure hope this won't take too long to end, and William and I are still standing to give these ladies the life they deserve.

Frank held out a letter and responded, "We aren't sure, but they left this."

"It was that damn Snake Pike. I just know it. His body will float the river tonight!" William definitely meant every word he said.

I tried my best to stay calm. I had known Mira for seven years and her family was a good hard working bunch. "William, give me a chance to read this letter. If it turns out it is Pike, we will take care of the matter how ever you see fit, as long as Mira comes home safe. I at least owe that to her mother and father."

I took the letter from Frank and read it. It simply said:

We took the first lady we saw from your town. If you want her to remain safe, Joshua William and Frank are to meet us due west of town at two-o-clock. All three or the deal is off and we keep the girl.

"Where did you find this letter?"

Frank spoke up. "We found it on one of the tables at the café. Dee, the owner of the place, said she didn't show up for work this morning. William and I went to her folks place to see if maybe she was ill. Her mother thought she was gone to work for the day. She said that she always gets up early to gather eggs and to get to Dee's to set all the tables for breakfast before anyone else arrives. Then we went back to the café and looked around to find the letter on one of the tables in the corner. It seems she knew that no one ever sat at that table, so she left it where it couldn't be thrown away or picked up by accident. She's a smart girl."

William chimed in, "We told her folks that we would get her back, Joshua. We have to. I swear every part of me

113

has never wanted more than to live a normal life with a pretty girl like that."

"William," I said. "We don't know for sure who wrote this. It may have been Pike. It may have been the gent that Louis ran out of town yesterday. I also found out this morning that old man Sterling has a son that went away East at a young age and got tied in with some ruthless people. He is supposed to return soon according to Mr. Sterling. The problem is, he's been gone so long that no one knows what he looks like anymore. He had left before I hired on at the ranch."

"I remember him," Frank said. "But, it has been a long, long time ago. If the old man doesn't know if he would recognize him, I wouldn't for sure."

"So you're telling me, I followed a track for five years to find the killer of the first woman I loved to get to a place where I have to go rescue another young lady that could've been taken by any number of men?"

"Yes, William. I guess that's what I'm telling you. I wish it were easier than that, but it's not. We don't know who this is we're dealing with." I tried to get through to my brother. He still had a strong love in his heart for family, Frank and I, and I was truly hoping he would realize that this time he wasn't alone with his trouble.

He stepped back and took a deep breath as Frank spoke. "William, I need to know how sure you are that the marked shoe belongs to the horse of the murderer. Are you sure this man you have followed is the person that killed Tom and Maggie?"

"When I rode up to that area where I found them, the trail was grown up pretty good. They weren't following a well-traveled trail. Of course, it's not like Tom had ever been west before. I sat in silence for a while after finding Maggie that way. Then I dug two graves. I marked them with the biggest rocks I could find and while I was doing that, I got mad. I got real mad. I found the first and only tracks I could and took out after the killer. After five years, I now know there may have been more than one man at that place. I just wanted to catch whoever had done that to Maggie, and here I am."

Frank looked at me and then to William. "Any of the three of us would have been just as mad, and would have done the same. Whoever did that to Maggie, had no idea the one man that would follow them to the end of the Earth would be the first man to find them. If he has any idea at all that you're on his trail, I bet he wishes now he hadn't done it at all."

"The problems at hand," I was trying to talk this out with Frank and William as well as work it out in my own head, "Are piling up on us. We are all three going to have to go west of town. I just wonder if this is part of the plan to get us out of town. Without us here, we are leaving the town wide open to trouble. If we don't all go, we may never see Mira again."

I was speaking when Louis had walked up. As soon as the words were out of my mouth, Louis spoke up.

"The town still has me. Charlie rode back in this morning, too."

"Turner is here also," William said. I know we just met him last night but I have a feeling we can count on him. With the three of them here, especially since most folks don't know about Turner yet, the town should be in good shape."

I had not thought that far ahead. Dalston is my town and all I am able to think is the fact that I don't want to be gone when it is attacked. I also know I have to get Mira back for William. If it was Ms. Kitchen, he'd help me. Frank would do anything for the two of us. I knew everyone was hoping for some great plan to come pouring out of my mouth. The only problem with that was, I didn't have one.

"Joshua," Louis said, "I will get in touch with Charlie and y'all find Turner. We will all meet at the café for lunch like normal. That should give us enough time to eat before you three need to ride out."

What a relief. Louis spoke up as if he were in charge of an entire troop of men. I never thought to ask if he was in the War. Most people didn't care about a man's past, or just didn't want to know. I don't guess a War where a country fights itself, and brothers kill brothers, is anything that needs to be brought back up. Some things you just let ride away into the past and you don't go hunting them up.

William spoke. He sounded a little calmer than he was a few moments before but there was still an anger, and sense of purpose in his voice. "I think I know where to find Turner. We can all meet at lunch."

"By the way Joshua," Frank said. "Who's the fellow in your jail? He's been raising hell all night and morning long and I see you didn't let him go yet."

"I'll explain later, Frank. I hope it's not related but it is another problem I have to face this evening. I'll see y'all later for a bite to eat at the cafe. I have some things to handle between now and then."

Louis walked toward home. It was still early and Mary would have been expecting him back. William went to the café. He always said coffee had a calming effect. That was exactly what he needed now. He needed to calm down a bit. Frank went his own way as he normally does. If he wasn't family, I would worry a lot more about his odd ways. I had work of my own to do. I had an idea that I didn't want to tell anyone about yet.

CHAPTER XIV

I really had no idea what to do at this time. Should I tell the others? Should I just handle my own affairs? What should I do? I really didn't know. I was seriously at a crossroads. If I chose the wrong path, the whole town could fall. My own blood could fall. My brother, the brother I hadn't seen in years, could fall. I couldn't let any of them down. All of this and I have to make it through safe to be with Ms. Kitchen. I have a lot of things to figure out.

I walked back into the jail to tell Dave I had things to take care of and I would arrange for someone to bring him lunch. I took a shotgun from the cabinet and grabbed a box of shells. My rifle was in the scabbard on the black, but having the street-sweeper made me feel better.

"No hard feelings sheriff. You are a fair man and I'm sorry I took a swing at you." Dave sounded concerned.

I turned towards him and replied, "No hard feelings Dave."

"I have only seen that look in a man's eyes once before in my whole life. I saw, and you may not believe me sheriff, William Mack in a small town years ago when I was young. He had been called out in the street by a man that was nowhere near as good as him. William got that same serious look in his eyes that you have right now."

"What happened that day, Dave?"

"William got called out by this man. I don't know if they had ever even met, sheriff but William didn't look like he was interested in killing anybody. He told the man so too. The man kept prodding even after William told him the last thing he wanted to do that day was kill this man in front of his son."

"His son?" I wasn't sure I was following Dave real well.

"Yeah. The man was with his son. The boy must have been twelve or thirteen. William explained to the man that he had watched his own pa die and wanted no part of a fight. The man just wouldn't take no for an answer and kept his hand right over his pistol."

"William never did hunt trouble. It just always seemed to find him. Did you get a name that day Dave?"

"I don't think that man ever said his name sheriff. What do you know about William? You talk like you know him." Dave was curious now and I wasn't sure I should have let that slip.

"William is my brother."

"That explains the look in each of your eyes. I've never seen any man more angry, or determined, or full of purpose in life. Until that day, I always thought William was just a story, a legend. He turned his back on the man to walk away. He couldn't have taken more than two or three steps when the man drew anyway. If you are half as fast as your brother, I'm glad I only took a swing at you. I'd of never got paid if I had to draw down on you."

I wasn't interested in compliments. "My brother is the most dangerous man I've ever met with a gun. What happened after that?"

121

"William must've heard the man slap leather. He spun fast and put two in the man's leg. I guess he was hoping to not have to kill him. That fella wouldn't take a hint. He started to raise his gun again and William had no choice. He finished the job. The son ran to his father's side and knelt, yelling the whole time that he would kill William. Just as he reached for the pistol, the marshal was there to grab it from the boy."

"I know William had a hard time with that. He was there the day Pa was shot." I couldn't remember that day the way I imagine William does. Maybe it's better that way.

Dave spoke up again. "William walked over and said, 'there's plenty of room in the Mississippi son, but I'll bet you'd like to bury your father. I'm sorry boy, but he wouldn't let it go. He left me no choice.' The young man stood up, looked up into William's eyes, and told him he'd kill him if it was the last thing he ever did on Earth."

"Thank you Dave. Maybe this boy is still alive, maybe he's already in the river. I will have your lunch brought and I will see you late in the afternoon to let you out."

"Sheriff, I'd say be safe but I am sure it'd be a wasted breath. The man or men, that are behind any trouble headed to Dalston, are in for a real surprise when they run up against you and your brother."

At that I left the jail to head to the Sterling ranch. I needed to talk to the old man. Before I left town, I walked over to the café to let Dee know that the man in my jail would need lunch brought to him. I told Dee what I needed to, and on my way out I saw William sitting over his coffee.

"William," I had to know, "do you remember killing a man in front of his son?"

"Yes, I do. That was a hard one to deal with. That was the last one before I decided to head west for a while to try and outrun my name. I know just how that boy felt that day."

"Do you think he could be on your trail?"

"The only man on my trail is Turner. But wait, he's about the right age for it to be him. It never crossed my mind the other night when we met. I do remember the boy whose father died in front of me and I killed the man that did it, but I have a hard time remembering either face, the boy or his father. The story Turner told happened after the other killing. It could be he was already on my trail. I had a few run ins on my way west. It was a good distance before men stopped recognizing me and trying their luck. I hope it's not him."

"I do too William. He seems like a decent man and we are leaving the town in his hands with Frank and Louis this afternoon." I was truly concerned now. We had to go get Mira back. We had no choice in the matter.

"I think Uncle Frank can handle anything that may come his way. I'll try to fill him in so he can at least be aware. You have that look in your eyes Joshua. What exactly do you have in mind?"

"I'm not sure brother, but I have to go see a few people before we ride. It's tough not knowing who or how many we are truly dealing with. I love this town and it all weighs heavy on me."

"Joshua," William became very serious and possibly a little sentimental, like he was the day we buried Pa, "We will figure all this out. This town will be going strong long after we're gone."

Just as I was heading out the door, a thought came to me. I spun on my heel and looked William dead in the eye. It had been an eternity since I had had so much to deal with and had my family, what was left of them, all here with me.

"William, I'm glad to have you back. I don't think I could do this on my own. I'll see you this afternoon when we ride."

At that, I walked out of the café and got on the big black. I checked the shotgun I had put in my spare scabbard and my rifle. I knew I might have needed every weapon I had before the day was through. I headed south out of town. I needed to talk to old man Sterling. He may not know much, but then again he may know more than he thinks. Sometimes, a man knows things that can help and doesn't even think about it. It is just like the story Dave told me about William. He may have never thought it could help. It's a shame I had to meet Dave the way I did. I know his wounds will heal but I kind of like him. He reminds me of every young cowhand. Honest for the most part, just trying to make an extra buck. You can't blame a man for trying to get ahead but he must also learn that a dishonest dollar will cost you.

I was not following the usual trail. There was a trail from the Sterling place that led to town. Then there was the path that the older hands used but, it wasn't used by many. This path led through the brush and trees. The main trail went straight across the plains. I wasn't looking to make myself a sitting target for anyone. Also, the old path was a good ride for the black. He always did like to get into the woods a little and weave his way through. I think he had seen enough of this flat Missouri land.

I wasn't pushing too hard. I had just come around a clump of oaks, thinking this could be as good a place as any for an ambush, when I saw him. He was a big man. He was clearing out as fast as he could and it caught my eye as to why. The man on the ground was barely moving, his horse standing a few yards away. I put the spurs to the black and thought for a moment about chasing the large man riding away before it occurred to me that I may be able to help the man left wounded. I rode straight to him and dismounted by his side. I saw the wounds before I had a chance to ask him if he was hit. It looked like he never got a chance to draw leather.

"You're the man from the bar last night." I realized he was the one that had taken a swing at Turner. He must have stayed the night in town and then headed back to the ranch this morning. He wasn't going to make it. You get a feel for wounds living in the West. "What happened?"

He talked with pain in his voice. "I was paid to come to town and take out that big man. His name was William Mack."

"Did you say William Mack?"

"Yeah. I was paid to come get William Mack out of the way for a while. Apparently, I swung that bottle at the wrong man, and it cost me my life. I should've never gone to town. I'm sorry sheriff. I never met any William. I was just thinking about the twenty dollars that man was offering me. You know how it is, with winter coming in a few months and all. I never meant to cause you any trouble."

"The trouble you're in is not anything that I can help. I wish all you had done was cause a fight in my town. You are riding toward the Sterling place. Do you work there?"

He was fading fast. "Yes sir, I hired on a few months back. The old man sure has a liking for you."

"I worked out on the ranch for some time before I took the sheriff's job."

This man looked as if he was near his last breath. I needed to know his name. "Tell me your name son. I will take your things to the ranch and get them to your family if I can."

"I got no family, sheriff. Ain't had any in a long time. That old man and a few of the hands are the closest thing to any family or friends I've ever had. Just make sure I get buried at the ranch. Please sheriff, that's all I want."

"I'll do it son." I felt bad for this young man. He was just another man trying to get ahead and winding up behind.

"My name is..." He stopped breathing just before he could tell me. I cleaned out his pockets and found no identification. All this man had on him was a few coins, a few bills and a pistol. I took all these and put them in my saddle bag. I took his horse and led him on to the ranch, constantly watching my trail and surroundings for the man that I knew had now offered to pay two men to come to town and fight. It was obvious to me that he wanted me and William out of the way. Both men came in last night for the job. He hadn't hired them to kill us, just to injure us and get us out of the way. He now knows that at least one man failed. The other man is in my jail. Could he possibly know that too?

Now I was confused. There was a man that had paid two men to take out William and me. Both came to do the job last night, meaning we were to be out of action for today. Today, we are being called out of town. If this man knows his hired help didn't succeed, he could have taken Mira out of town. That would have taken some incredible planning. Maybe we are dealing with two separate men. This entire ordeal was getting completely out of hand. I had to ride on to the ranch and see Sterling.

CHAPTER XV

I rode into the yard of the ranch. There were hands in the corral breaking horses. It brought back memories for me of when I worked on the place. Though so much had happened already today, it was only just past ten. I needed to speak to Sterling and get back to town. I dismounted the black at the hitching rail in front of the main house. Samuel was sitting on the front porch, picking his teeth with a stick he had obviously whittled down for that purpose.

"It's good to see you sheriff," he said as he stood to greet me. I still wasn't sure about this strange man. I had a feeling, after our meeting on my front porch this morning that he was an honest man, one who's words I could trust. But, with the things going on right now around town, I could never be sure. Pa always told us that a man isn't always what he seems and you can't trust anyone but family.

"It's nice to see you again, Samuel. I came to see the old man."

"He's not feeling too well this morning and has asked me not to bother him."

I felt a little feeling of distrust with Samuel at that moment. Maybe he just hasn't been around long enough to know the relationship Sterling and I had. He was like a father to me when I went to work for him. My pa was gone, and my brother was making his own way, and I found a home on the ranch. I worked harder than any man he had. I did everything I could to keep the operation running. I had no family other than Frank and William, and Sterling gave me a place to call home. I wanted someday to have my own place like this. All that ended the day I went to town to take care of the Sloan boys. I've been sheriff ever since and had the responsibility of protecting Dalston.

I looked the man in the eyes and responded sternly, "Tell the old man that Joshua Mack is here."

Samuel looked at me like he wished I would just leave. I wasn't sure if he was just doing his job or if maybe he really didn't want me around. He had no choice, because he could tell I wasn't leaving, and he turned to go tell Mr. Sterling I was here. Just as he was headed to the door, some of the older hands, the ones that had been there when I was, were headed to the porch to say hello to me. He went inside and I turned my attention to them.

"Howdy, Clint, how's thing's been going" I said as Clint Tucker was walking up to me. He was an average man with a big heart. He looked after me when I was young.

"Joshua," Clint spoke and I realized suddenly how long it had been since I had been out to the ranch to see the boys. He reached the porch and extended his hand to me. We shook hands like old friends before I asked him my first question.

"How are things here on the ranch, Clint? Is everything running normal?"

"Well, me and the older boys aren't sure how to take the hiring of this Samuel. We have never been men to question the old man's decisions, but this new man is an odd one. He seems like he has Sterling's intentions in mind. We just aren't sure."

131

"I'm not sure either Clint." I wasn't sure. I wanted to stand and talk to Clint and the men for a while, but the old man came busting out the door. He looked perfectly healthy to me. Was Samuel trying to keep me from seeing him? Was he really a little under the weather and maybe my presence gave him enough life to get out of bed? There were so many questions going through my mind.

"Joshua Mack, the best man I ever had for breaking horses." Sterling said it and I knew he meant it.

"Hello, old man." It had been a while.

"I'm not near as old as you think of me Joshua. I'm still getting along just fine. Wish I had two or three of you here on the ranch and things would be better." He was looking just as spry as he ever did.

"Sterling," I always just called him Sterling or old man, "Can we go somewhere and talk, just me and you?"

"Sure we can boy. I always have time for you."

At that, we stepped inside. On the way in the door, Sterling stopped Samuel and told him he'd be fine. We walked in the main room and I immediately went to the parlor and poured myself a drink. I guess that was enough of a clue for the old man.

"What's eating at you Joshua?"

"I have a lot on my plate and I'm afraid I may have to eat it all before I know exactly what I'm dealing with."

"I know how you feel. Word has reached me that my son is headed back home. As you probably know, I have wanted him back here with me for a long time. The only problem is, the way I know he is returning is he wrote me a letter. It said that he was coming back to take over. I have no problem running this ranch, and I have been informed that he got in with a tough, power-hungry crowd out east. I have the feeling that he is coming back to unseat his old man. I am afraid, Joshua."

I wished I could settle the old man's nerves but I had too much going on to know what to say. "I will do everything I can to protect your ranch and my town. I have my brother and Uncle Frank at my side." It was very comforting to know I had my family at my side.

"I had heard your brother was back in town." Sterling said it with a feeling of relief and surprise at the same time. "He was a good man with a gun. Good enough to build a legend around."

"Yes sir. William is back. That is why I am here to see you. I am truly sorry that it took some trouble headed to Dalston to get me to come out and visit. I should've ridden out to see you long before all this."

"Don't worry Joshua," he said it as he was pouring himself a drink. "I know you are busy keeping the town in order and I know you have a thing for that Kitchen girl."

"I didn't know that anybody knew how I feel about her." I was confused to say the least.

"I know you better than you think, Joshua. Remember you spent a lot of time on my place as a youngster. I have seen you a few times while I was in town. You have the same look in your eyes for her that I had for my wife. She's been gone a long time but I will never forget that feeling or that look." Old man Sterling knew things and kept up with me a lot more than I knew.

"I intend to marry her, and not be sheriff anymore, if I can pull the town through the trouble that is headed our way. I have a few questions for you. Do you mind if I ask?" I knew he didn't mind answering any of my questions but I thought I would ask since it had been forever since I had seen the old man.

"I can answer any question you have Joshua. If I don't know the answer, I will do what I can to find out. You are more like a son to me than anybody.

I knew he meant what he was saying. I had been very close to Mr. Sterling after my father's death and his son had been gone since before that. I always felt that of any of the people in the town of Dalston, other than my uncle and my brother, I could always count on Sterling.

"Are you missing any men, Sterling?"

"I am. Clint told me that Dave and Matt have been gone since yesterday evening. I was a little worried, but, I have seen men for years make a little money and move on. Do you have any idea what happened to them, Joshua?"

I wasn't sure how to tell him so I just laid it on the line. "Dave is in my jail back in town and the other man, the one you called Matt, is about a mile or so from here on the old path to town."

"He's in jail?" Sterling spoke as if he couldn't believe Dave could ever do any wrong. "And Matt is dead?"

"Yes Sterling. One man is dead and another in jail. It seems they were both paid, possibly by the same man, to come to town and take me and William out. Neither of them were instructed to draw on us. They were just told to fight us and injure us. They didn't succeed. Dave took a swing at me and took quite a whipping last night and I threw him in jail. Matt, I assume, rode an incredibly wonderful looking paint?"

"He did have a beautiful looking paint. He was proud of that horse."

"Well old man," I spoke as clearly as I could. I was trying to work all this out in my head as well as tell him what I knew about his men and what happened to them. "I was riding out here this morning to see you about everything going on, and I found Matt dying on the trail. There was a man riding away but I thought I would be able to help your man. He was hit hard and there was no help for him. I spoke to him until he died. You should send someone to get him. He seemed to me like a decent young man. He needs a proper burial."

Mr. Sterling looked as if he knew how I felt. He knew that young men sometimes made bad decisions. I was very thankful that I had listened to the old man when I was working on the ranch. He had been in the West for a long time, just as Pa had. Hard work, and listening to those that came before us, had taught a lot of us to be the men we turned out to be. We were truly lucky we listened.

"He was a young man," Mr. Sterling said. "He just hired on a few months back and seemed like one of the boys that were just trying to make a few dollars before he moved on. I'm sorry you had to find him that way and I'm sorry any of my men would ride to town to make trouble for you."

"They weren't much trouble really. Turner, a new man in town, took care of Matt. It seems the only description Matt was given was a big man, new to town. He thought Turner was that man. William was the man he was supposed to attack. Turner is a big man, like William, but I think he made a lucky mistake. Otherwise, William may have killed him last night. He gained one more day with his mistake. Dave got the man he was told to fight. It was me but, I was in no mood for a fight. I whipped him quickly and threw him in a cell."

Old man Sterling poured us both another drink. I wasn't normally much of drinker but I had a lot to deal with and the old man was always easy to drink with. I took the drink in hand and, with no intention of drinking all of it, took a sip. The old man walked nervously across the room before he spoke another word.

"Do you think they are both involved in this whole thing Joshua? They were good hands here on the ranch. My boy has me really worried."

"I don't think either of them knew what they were getting into. I'm not sure your son is involved either. I wish I could tell you he was not a part of this but I'm not so sure. All I know for sure," I was talking to the old man like I was talking myself through all of this, "All I know for sure is that William and Frank are on my side and we have trouble heading our way. I'm not sure who is in charge of the men that are my trouble, but I know we have no choice but to figure it out. William has the look of a man in over his head when he is around Mira, the girl that serves you at Dee's, and I need to get through all of this alive so I can make an honest woman of Ms. Kitchen. She is the only lady I have ever loved."

Sterling looked me in the eye. "I'll send Clint to get Matt's body and bring him back to the ranch to be buried. He said he had no family when he hired on."

"He told me the same thing. He just trusted the wrong man. I have some more business to handle before I get back to town to release Dave. He said he was to meet the man that offered to pay him to take me out. Now that Matt has been killed, I'm worried about letting Dave go to collect his money. Perhaps Matt was killed for going for the wrong man. Perhaps he was killed because the man hiring the two men never had any intention of paying either man. I'll do what I can to get Dave back out here to the ranch safely. Lord knows I don't want to see any other man die for all this trouble."

Sterling knew how I felt. "I hope no one else has to die before all this is through Joshua. I can hope all I want but I feel like there is a ton more trouble headed our way and more deaths to come. I just truly hope that you nor your brother, or anyone for that matter, has to kill my son when he returns."

"I hope so too, old man. If your son is the man behind all this, and I pray he's not, neither William nor I will hesitate to kill him. I know he's your blood but I have a town to protect. I will not let any man stand in the way of me doing my job. I also won't let anything stand in the way of my brother and I coming through this alive."

CHAPTER XVI

I had asked the old man if I could ride around a bit before I left. Of course, he never had a problem with me being on the ranch and none of the boys would think twice about seeing me out and about. I went out to mount up and Clint walked over to me.

"Is everything okay, Joshua?"

"Yeah, I think so. Being here on the ranch is the best I've felt in a day or two. I wish right now I was headed over to that corral to show them youngsters how it's done. Has anything been going on out here out of the ordinary, other than Samuel?" I knew if there was any small detail, Clint would know. He had a memory no one could match.

"We have been seeing some odd tracks left out on the range. They're made by shoes no one around here has ever seen,"

"Clint," I was hoping to get a no for an answer, "Do they have a six on one side and a gun on the other?"

"How'd you know that, Joshua? I know you haven't been out in while."

"Well, it turns out, that is the man my brother, William, has been following. He said he found the tracks at the scene where Tom and Maggie were killed. He's been on that trail for five years and it has led him back here to Dalston."

"Tom and Maggie are dead? That must have been hard on William. I know your brother was in love with that girl and stepped out of the way so she could have a good life with Tom. You said he was back here, in town?"

140

"Yes. William followed those same hoof prints back to here. He is in town and I'm glad to have him."

"Joshua, do you know whose horse those shoes belong to?"

"No. We haven't figured that out yet but since you told me that, I don't need to take a ride around the ranch. I know the old man has been worried about his son coming back. You were here when he was a kid. Do you honestly think he could have changed that much from being raised here?"

Clint looked at the ground and kicked some dirt. He then looked up at me and responded, "I know when he was a young man, he was the exact copy of his old man. Wherever the old man went, he went. He even talked just like him. But, when his mother died, he was very angry with everybody and everything. Sterling thought it best to send him East to get an education. The boy didn't argue. It was almost as if he were happy to get away from a place that had brought him so much pain. You never can tell how being in a new place and around different folks will affect a man. I would like to think, and have for a long time, that he would come back and run this ranch for his old man."

"William has been gone for sixteen years. The only thing I can tell that has changed about him is he is faster than ever. Time and surroundings can change a man if he lets it. How did Sterling come to think his son was coming back, and does he have reason to believe he has gone bad?"

"Well Joshua, he got a letter a while back from an associate of his in Boston that his boy was taking up with some ruthless men and talking about coming home to take over his father's place. The old man has hoped for the best, but prepared for the worst. That is why he hired Samuel. Just to protect him. He wants us to handle the cows and he wants Samuel to handle everything else."

I still wasn't too certain about this Samuel character. He seemed straight but a man never knows.

"Don't trust him Clint. Just watch out for Sterling and hopefully with me and William and Frank, the town and this ranch will make it through."

"I haven't trusted him since he arrived but I have yet to tell the old man that."

"No need to. If he ever gets a feeling that Samuel is in the wrong, he'll let us know. Just watch over things here and I will do my best to figure the rest out. Thanks for the talk Clint. When this is all over, I may have to come back and show them youngsters how to handle a horse."

"That'd be a sight Joshua. That'd be a sight."

"I'm going back to town to let Dave out of jail. Sterling will fill you in on what's going on. I'll send him right back here this afternoon. Hope he makes it. I'll be seeing you Clint."

At that, I got on the black and rode out of the yard. One look back let me know that Samuel was concerned with my visit. He was near the barn watching like a hawk, too afraid to interfere. It is possible that he is just the man that Sterling needed here, but we here in the west always have our doubts until a man shows who he really is. I had a few more answers now. Though I never met him, I really hoped for Sterling's sake, that his son wasn't involved in any of this.

I rode from the ranch along the main trail. I wasn't afraid of seeing the dead man again because I had seen plenty. I just learned at a young age not to follow the same path too much and there was the big man to worry about now. South of Dalston, on this trail, was a mighty lonely place to find myself. I could tell it was getting close to eleven or twelve because it was starting to heat up and a time or two I had to stop and clear the sweat from my brow.

It was at one of those stops that I saw them. It was the tracks we all had in mind by now, a six and a gun. The man that horse belonged to had crossed the trail here. He apparently had stopped for a moment, possibly to see if he was followed or not. It's funny how growing up in the west lets you learn so much from a track or two.

The tracks were headed from the west to the east. Now west of here could lead anywhere, but I figure almost due east of here was the old path where Matt still laid. These were the only tracks I had seen before getting close to the ranch. These tracks belonged to the big man that killed Matt. Everything seemed to come back to these damn tracks. If we could just place the man the tracks belonged to.

As I rode on I got to thinking. We thought the tracks had belonged to Snake Pike at first but Pike was an average man at best. The man I saw leaving the scene at Matt's death was a larger man. That of course doesn't clear Pike from being involved in this mess. Pike is clearly a concern with Charlie and the Marshalls giving us so much detail about their operation. They have been a serious problem for quite a few towns along the trail.

Foster Grant, Pike's employer and head of the herd passing through, seemed like a wise old man that just wanted to push some cows. He did keep us from gunplay when William and I were out at the herd. It's probably him that has kept any of his men from coming to town and causing trouble. Of course Pike and his men could just be waiting for the right moment. According to Charlie, they always push the herd through the town and then Pike's men ride in, after he has told them the layout, and rob the town blind. I realized at this time, Pike was not my concern, unless the big man worked for him. That seemed unlikely seeing as how William had been following the man with the marked horse shoes for five long years.

As I was thinking this through in my mind, at a calm trot back towards town, I realized the hunch I had earlier to go check up on the herd, and Pike, was useless until we knew more. At that moment I decided to look at my watch. It was pushing noon and I was still a few miles from town. If I picked up the pace, I could still make lunch at the café and talk to William and Frank, if they were around, about what I had learned today. I still had some concern about Turner.

I rode up to town to see everything was as usual. I had seen no other tracks on the main trail to the ranch other than the six gun horseshoes. This was a good clue that the big man that rode that horse was the only man that could definitely be involved in any of this. That man was the man that paid Matt, and then killed him.

CHAPTER XVII

When I got to town, I don't know why, but I rode straight to Emily's store. I had a feeling that I needed to see her. I tied the black to the hitching rail and stepped on the boardwalk only to find the door locked. What was I thinking? She always closed shop at lunch time. I turned to walk to the café. When I entered I found a seat saved at the table with Frank, William and Turner. I spoke to Dee and found lunch hadn't been delivered to my prisoner, Dave. I asked Dee to fix two plates and I would take one to. He could leave mine at the table. I'd just be a few minutes.

I walked to the table. "Boys, I'll be right back in a few minutes. I'm gonna take some food to the jail."

"We'll be here," William said. With everything going on around here, it was good to even hear a small thing like that from my brother.

I took the plate from Dee and left to cross the way to the jail. When I arrived, Dave was ready to eat a horse.

"Thought you had forgot to tell anyone to feed me sheriff. Of course we've all gone a day or two without but I was getting hungry. Thanks for the lunch," he said as he took the plate of beef and beans.

"Listen Dave," I wasn't exactly sure how to tell him all this. "You go on and eat and I'm gonna leave the cell open so you are free to go when you're done. You must make me one promise though."

"Anything you say sheriff. Seems you are the straightest man I have ever met. The boys at the ranch and the old man are right about you."

146

I looked Dave dead in the eyes when I spoke because I needed him to take in every word as important. "I'm letting you go with twenty dollars that was given to me this morning by a friend of yours. It seems Matt was paid by the same man you were. He was to come in and pick a fight with my brother, William. All I can figure is this man, whoever he may be, wanted us both out of the way, or just banged up. Matt met him this morning on the old path to the ranch and the man shot him twice in the gut and left him for dead. I came along just before he died and he told me everything and gave me the money the man paid him and asked I give it to you. He said he wanted you to have his so you wouldn't go to try and collect yours."

"Matt is dead?" I could tell he was shaken.

"Yes. I'm asking you to ride straight to the ranch when you're done eating. Clint was going out to get the body. You are not to go to the bend of the river tonight to collect your money. I will have to figure out who this man is and I will take care of it. Just go to the ranch and stay for a few days. Are we understood?"

"Yes sheriff. Did Matt really say he wanted me to have his money?"

Matt had said no such thing, but I kind of figured if I told Dave that, I had a better chance of getting him to go to the ranch to stay. I didn't need another of Sterling's men dead.

"Yes, Dave, he did. The man that shot him was fast, Matt never cleared leather. Now eat and go back to the ranch." I left him to his meal and headed back to the café to

147

join William and get a bite in me. As I crossed the street I saw Ms. Kitchen returning to her store and gave her a polite nod. I always have loved the way she stops to watch me walk by. It makes me feel wanted. I hope to make it past all this so I can show her just how much she is wanted.

Walking in the café, I realized I needed to eat in a hurry so we could get on our way soon. Frank and William were talking casually of the places William had been in the years he was gone. William went on and on about how beautiful the country out in Colorado was. He said he found a little vein and mined it until it played out and when he cashed in his gold, he had enough put aside that he hasn't had to worry about working for the five years he's been following the man he's after. I was aware that Frank had drawn him into small talk to keep him calm. Normally William was the calmest man I knew, other than Pa, but the fact that the girl he wanted had been taken put an angry edge on William. Turner was too involved with his food to chime in.

I sat down and ate quickly, only stopping to nod at William's story now and then. When I finished my plate, I paid Dee for all the meals, even Dave's, and we four men stepped outside to face the day. It seemed I had already had a full day but there was plenty more I needed to handle. We stood side by side by side by side, all hoping to make it through the trouble ahead. No one spoke as we checked our weapons and mounted up.

Turner was busy with his pistol when William gave me a wink and said, "We thought with Charlie and Louis in town, Turner should ride with us." I knew what he meant. There was little trust to be formed in one night and, the story

Dave told got us all wondering if Turner was the good kid, or the bad one that wanted to kill William.

Once saddled, we headed out of town, due west. I had a feeling that any man wanting to meet someone out west of town probably wanted to do so at the old cabin. There was an old cabin that had been out on the p ains, lined on one side by a nice group of oak and pecan. We never knew who had built it but they had done a fine job, for it had been standing long before any of us had been .

"We heading to the cabin?" Frank and William almost spoke at the same time.

"Yes we are. I figure that's where I would hole up if I were inviting men to come meet me west of town."

"What's the cabin?" Turner was obviously curious.

"Due west of town a ways, there is an old cabin that was built long ago. It has the most solid, thick walls around and has stood longer than any structure I've seen in my days. If Joshua thinks that is where we should go, then that is where we go." Frank always said he trusted my instincts. He said I got them from my father and Pa was never wrong. It is a shame he wasn't with us. I couldn't remember thinking that way for years.

I needed to let Turner know how this was to all go down. "Turner," I spoke and he rode up beside me.

"Yes sir sheriff?"

"We will come upon a bluff in a mile or two. At that bluff, you will need to ride north for a ways until you hit the

149

tree line and then you can turn west and follow the trees and they will naturally turn southwest and bring you up on the backside of the cabin. The note said for the three of us, William, Frank and I to come. I'm worried if we bring a fourth out in the open, Mira could be hurt. The only thing we are riding out to accomplish today is to get Mira back home safe."

"Understood, Joshua. I'll stay out of sight until I am either needed or I know for certain everything is good."

"Thanks. Turner, it's nice to have another man by my side to help protect this town." Turner was a difficult book to read but I was hoping we really could count on him.

"I follow William, sheriff, wherever he goes and whatever he does." The words sure sounded authentic and I looked to Frank and William. They both nodded in approval. This made me feel better for the time being. We were approaching the bluff and just as told, Turner turned north.

"See ya'll after this is over," he said as he rode away from the group.

"I really want to believe he is with us, William," I talked as we rode up on top of the bluff.

"I know what you mean, Joshua, and I don't blame you for being stingy with your trust. Pa taught us not to trust anybody at face value and it has kept both of us alive many times if I had to guess.

"We can trust him as long as he doesn't give us a reason not to." Frank said the words as the cabin came into sight in the distance. We pulled up and I looked to William and Frank.

"If the shooting starts, just do your best to get the girl out safe. Remember she's what we came for, not the man that took her. If I go down, just get that girl back to her family safe." I pulled out the shotgun as I spoke.

"You brought the shotgun? You must be worried," Frank said.

"I just want to get this over with. No shooting unless fired upon or forced. Let's go boys."

We rode slowly, three wide and spread out a ways toward the cabin. There were two horses tied up on the side of the cabin by a water trough. There was a window or two broken in the front of the old place but it still stood strong. If a man were to fire on us now, we'd be sitting targets. Our ammo would never go through those walls, not to mention we can't just shoot blindly into a building with Mira inside.

What happened next happened so fast it was a blur. William was checking all around as a man like him must do to stay alive as long as he had. He looked down once and saw them. Tracks leading the same way as ours were made by a horse wearing six-gun shoes. William instantly dismounted, about the same time mine and Frank's eyes caught what he was looking at and he was walking straight toward the cabin when the door opened. A man, a very large well-built man, walked out the door. He came out saying something about being happy we had come when William drew his pistol.

"No William," I yelled just as I caught up to him and knocked his arms into the air, sending the bullet from his weapon into the air over the cabin. Frank had the man covered and he was stunned by the speed of my brother's draw. He wasn't about to go anywhere near his pistol.

"He's the man I've been hunting and today he answers for what he's done!" William meant it too.

"He came out without Mira and we have to know where she is before we do anything." I was worried about the girl first. I was also confused that a man would call the three of us out here and walk right out into the open without so much as drawing his pistol.

At my words about Mira, she walked out of the cabin with a smile on her face and completely unharmed.

"Did he harm you in any way Mira?" William asked with concern for her, but I could tell and I think Frank could too, that he was just looking for a reason to kill this man. I felt his need to end all of this. I just wasn't sure this was the way.

"Oh," she spoke so sweetly. "Adam came to me this morning and asked if I would help him. He wanted to be able to get the three of you out of town, so he could speak to you without anybody knowing he was here. When he said he was old man Sterling's son, I had no worry about coming with him. He hasn't hurt me in any way."

I stepped forward and said, "You're Sterling's son?"

"Yes sir. Thank you for not letting him shoot me. I had no intention of anyone getting hurt with this plan of mine. If Mira hadn't agreed to come with me, I would have reached you another way."

William had lowered his weapon but still had plenty of anger built up and questions to ask. "I need to know where you were five years ago."

"Excuse me sir?"

"My name is William Mack and I need to know where you were five years ago. I need to know now!"

Adam was shocked. You could tell he thought he was in the clear now that Mira was outside speaking to us. "Five years ago," he paused to think. "Five years ago I was in Colorado near Denver. Why does that matter mister?"

By the time he was asking his last question, William was already raising his pistol again. I reached his arms once more just in time to stop him from killing this man.

"William," Frank finally had something to offer. "William, this man is scared out of his head and has not once threatened us or the girl. Think about it nephew. Stay calm and let's talk this through. I have a feeling there will be plenty of killing to come soon. Just put away your piece now. I've got him covered."

William looked at me and Frank, not mad or upset but calmly. This was good. He then looked back to Sterling's boy and said coldly, "Adam, is that what you said your name was?"

"Yes sir, it is."

"If I find you are the man I have been hunting for five years, I will have to apologize to your father after I throw your body in the Mississippi. "

"You are that William Mack? The William Mack? I almost got killed by a man believed to be one of, if not the, fastest man in the West." Adam spoke with such awe and surprise. I had a feeling that maybe he had no clue what the significance of his horse's shoes meant.

"Frank," I turned to him. "You should let Turner know it's safe to come out of those woods." Frank turned and sent a whistle and a wave into the groups of trees. Turner came riding out a moment later. He had hidden well because we didn't see him until he got right to the tree line.

William looked to Mira. "Please forgive me for my actions and words ma'am."

"I would forgive you for all the evil in the world, William Mack. I don't think you are near the bad man this world has made you out to be." She still spoke soft and sweet. Frank and I looked at each other and knew right then, if we all made it through this, William was a goner. She wanted him like he wanted her and that can be a dangerous combination.

William turned up a big smile to her and turned back to Sterling's boy with a stern face. He was calmed but still wanted answers. "How long have you been riding horses with shoes that have a six on one side and a gun in the other?"

"I've put those on my horses since I won a shooting championship in New York. I outshot every man in New York, at least the ones that showed up for the competition. The people I was associated with, after my schooling, were not good folks and they found that I could shoot well. They had me built up to be a bad man in the city. I tried to explain to them that there were men in the west that would kill me before I could draw. They didn't believe me. They don't even believe the dime novels. They think William and the Kid are stories."

William still wanted to know why the shoes had been such a clue for him for so long. I had not had the chance to tell William and Frank of the tracks I saw this morning on the way back from the ranch. I had a question myself.

"Adam, I am Joshua Mack, sheriff of the town of Dalston."

"My father sent me a letter, years ago, telling me about you and how you had taken out the Sloan bunch single-handedly. He said you were quite a man and the town was plenty safe, having you as sheriff." That sounded just like something the old man would write.

"I found tracks this morning, southwest of here that match those of your horse. Can you explain that?"

William spoke up, "You never mentioned that to us."

"I haven't had time brother. Until we got here and saw the same tracks, I didn't think there was any way it was the same man."

Adam stepped forward and said, "It wasn't the same man. I've been here with Mira since just after dawn."

"He has. We have been visiting and he hasn't gone any farther than the trough to get water for coffee. He even brought some cured ham and bread to eat for lunch. He's been right here with me."

I was now more confused than I had ever been. I had a thought. I couldn't believe it had never occurred to me before. Not many men would ever mark their shoes the same as another man. You never wanted to be in the situation that Adam Sterling was in right now, with us thinking he was guilty of something he didn't do. Maybe my idea was correct.

"Adam, why did you want us out here?"

"I needed to let you know I was back but didn't want anyone else to know. I couldn't just ride out to the ranch or down the main street to announce myself. I left the east a long time ago, but there are men that I was associated with that tried to convince me a few times to come back and take over father's ranch. I know I left at a bad time and was raised up in the east, but my father is my father. I could never betray him."

"How do you think I found your tracks near a murder this morning? It was a murder of one of your father's men that had been paid to come to town last night to try William. Not with guns though, just to try and hurt him. There were actually two men offered twenty apiece. One was to try William and the other to injure me." I tried to keep everything clear as I spoke.

William spoke up, "A man came to fight me?"

"Yes William. He was told there was a large man, new to town, and he was to try to hurt him. No guns, just injure him. He obviously saw Turner and thought he had the right big man. This morning, after taking a whipping from

156

Turner last night, he was heading back to the ranch and met the man that paid him along the way. He was then shot twice in the gut and left for dead. I found him on the way out to see Clint and the old man this morning."

Adam finally responded. "I have been here all morning with the girl. I promise sheriff. I really wish I could go see my father. Are you sure it was my tracks?"

"You have a six on one side and a gun on the other. That's what I found." As I said it I walked over nearer his horse and squatted down. The thought I had was correct. I looked up to Adam and said, "Have you always marked your shoes the same exact way?"

"Yes sheriff, I have. Since I won that competition I have marked them with a six, read in the direction I'm riding, and the word gun, also read down the way I was riding. I figured that way, if a man wanted to follow me, he had plenty of warning he could read before he got to me."

"That explains why I found the tracks this morning, while you were here with Mira. The tracks I found are the opposite of yours. The tracks I found this morning, also from a horse ridden by a big man such as you, were facing the other way. Someone, and I wish I knew who, knows your shoe and is trying to set it up like you are responsible for everything going on right now."

It must have occurred to William that this was possible and he was digging through the images in his mind. He finally spoke up, "The tracks I found at Maggie and Tom's death were just like yours. I have followed them for five years and I should know exactly what they look like. How do you explain that?" William was still angry about the man that killed Maggie.

"You have followed me since Colorado, five years ago?" Adam looked concerned but not worried.

"Yes. I rode out of the hills to find a girl I knew from my younger days, one I was very fond of, and her husband, dead." William looked to Mira to see if any jealousy appeared. She seemed to be just taking it all in and sent a shy smile back to William, as if to say, 'I still love you.'

Adam didn't waste any time explaining. "I must have been right in front of you on that trail. I was riding along and found the dead man first. Then I found the girl, in bad shape and dead, from a shot to the head."

I was glad he just described it as 'in bad shape.' I didn't believe a young pretty girl like Mira needed to hear the details.

Adam continued. "I would have stayed and buried them, but I was close enough to hear the shots. I stopped just long enough to see they were both dead and I took out after the killer. When I knew I wasn't going to catch him, but had a good idea of how to keep his trail, I turned to go back. When I got close I saw a man, that must have been you, William, looking at the tracks I had left. I didn't want to have to explain that away."

"So you just rode away?" William was curious at this point. He had just told me and Frank that he wasn't sure those were the only tracks at Maggie's death, just the only ones he knew he could follow.

"For five years," Adam said, "I have followed the man responsible."

Frank laughed a little and said, "You mean you have been following a murderer, William has been following you, and Turner has been on William's trail? On top of all that, this five year ride has brought you all back here, to Dalston, William's home town. There isn't a soul in the world that could have even thought that possible."

CHAPTER XVIII

The words had just cleared Frank's mouth. Turner was on the ground, hit, before any of us heard the shot ring out. I glanced at Frank to see he was moving to the cabin. William broke into a dead run, picking up Mira on his way, and was through the door with Frank not far behind. I ran to Turner, who was getting up on his own, to see if he was injured. The next shot hit the ground at our feet as Turner and I were stepping into the door of the old cabin. The door was slammed behind us by Mira. She seemed calmer than any of us. I guess as a lady, you are less apt to be shot at. All of the men in this room had been shot at plenty to know when to be afraid.

We could hear our horses scatter. William was already at the window, asking if anyone had brought a rifle inside. I was checking on Turner. He had taken a bullet in the arm. It looked like it just grazed him and he said as much. It seemed no one had a rifle. The rifles were still all in our scabbards. If the men shooting wanted, they could stay just out of pistol distance and take shots into the cabin. Just as I thought about that, we heard a big deep voice from the top of the bluff we had just ridden over.

"Don't try to follow. All but the two horses tied up are scattered and if I'm followed, I will shoot every last one of you. We'll meet again soon enough." The voice didn't sound perfectly natural. It was almost familiar, and a little disguised. Maybe the man was hollering through a bandana. I had seen it done before to change a man's voice just so it wouldn't be recognized.

William and Frank were at the front windows with me, watching the rider clear the hill. Mira had torn a piece of cloth from the bottom of her dress and started to bandage Turner's arm.

"How long do ya'll want to wait?" Frank sounded truly angry.

"I say we give it a few minutes and then gather the horses Frank." I wanted to give chase too, but was trying to think as clearly as a tired man could. I was so tired for it to be this early in the day, but then again, I had lived about a month's worth of cowboy time in the past few days.

"Damnit I'm for going after him now!" Frank was mad.

William responded to Frank's outburst. "No Frank, Joshua is right. We have had enough action for now and we have a lady with us to worry about."

Frank lowered his voice with his response. "You're both right. We may have more trouble from whoever shot before we get to town, and Mira is our priority."

That put a smile on William's face. He knew we both could plainly tell how he felt for her. Frank rolled a smoke and lit up, almost as if to say that was how long we were going to wait.

"My arm is a little sore but I'm fine. Just flesh, that's all. I'll go gather the horses. Thank you Mira for fixing me up." Turner didn't even have to be here with us and he was the man shot. At least now, we knew he was with us and not just playing the part. A shot like that was too risky to fake. He couldn't have anything to do with the man on the hill.

163

I felt the need to speak up, after all I was the first one to doubt this man that just took a shot for us and was now willing to be the first outside. "I'll go with you Turner. Adam, you should come along. The three of us can fetch those horses pretty quick. If Turner can get his, I'll get one and you get the other."

Adam looked puzzled until we opened the door to step out. He had to be thinking I had mentioned finding three horses and there were four of us that hadn't tied up. When we opened the door and stepped out, the black was standing right next to Adam's and Mira's horses.

"Go figure," William said with a laugh. "You always did have the best horse around. Hell, even that ugly little bag of bones you used to ride when we were kids would wait out a tornado for you."

"Pa always told me that women and horses were a lot alike. If you treat them right, pet them, and make sure they got food to eat, they will do just about anything for a man." I had almost forgotten Mira was with us. I looked to her, half embarrassed and half for approval.

"Well Joshua Mack," she spoke so softly. "I don't know much about horses but I would say that is pretty true with women." At that last comment, she turned to check on her horse, the one she didn't know much about, obviously to let her response settle deep into William and I.

Adam, Turner and I went and got our horses. They weren't scattered too far. The three of them had gotten just shy of the tree line behind the house, which wasn't far away. Adam still looked to be in shock from this whole experience.

He had to have known that taking a girl from our town was going to get us riled, but he never imagined it would almost get him shot and killed.

He asked me on the way back to join the others, "He was really going to shoot me, wasn't he?"

I had no tender way to put it and this was not a time for tender words anyway. "Yes. Any man in his shoes, following you for that long, would have. William is not a bad man, don't get that wrong. He is the best I've known since pa died."

"I have to say the same exact words Joshua," Turner added. "If not for William killing the man that murdered my father, I don't know where I would have been. I almost lost his trail a few times over the years but after he left that vein in Colorado, I picked up the bits he had left and have had enough to keep up. Of course money wasn't the issue then. I had had to do odd jobs here and there before that to make a little, and sell a few of my family's things, to keep up since then. After that, the money was there but William rode with such a purpose. I always knew when he caught up with the man responsible, that man was in for it. Now I know why and it all makes since. I'll be glad for the both of you when this is all over."

Adam was moved by what all had gone on. He looked several times as if he wanted to speak but was careful with his choice of words. He finally stumbled on some that couldn't possibly hurt. "Sheriff, how is my father? I mean, you said you went to see him this morning right?"

"I was at the ranch this morning. Your father is fine. He seems in good spirits and good health." I didn't want to tell him that his letter had worried the old man and he had hired Samuel.

We walked up to the cabin to join William, Frank, and Mira. We all mounted up, William helping Mira onto her horse. I told the group that I would ride out ahead to make sure the man that had fired on us wasn't lying in wait to take another shot. A few of the boys argued at first but I told them it had to be me. Dalston was my town. They finally gave up arguing with me and I rode out in the lead.

I got to the top of the bluff and saw some tracks. I got down just long enough to examine them. Sure enough, they were the same tracks, the reverse of Adam's own, that I had seen when I found Matt that morning. I didn't want to wait on them to catch up so I turned to the group. All I had to do was point to the ground and I knew they knew what I meant. I moved on. It did appear that the tracks were heading at a fast pace away from us. That man knew that with us having a lady with us, we would take his warning and lay off. He was right and it seemed we would have a clear ride back to town.

William was in the lead when the group reached the edge of town safely, catching up to me.

"Joshua, I never thought you would have the good eye of the family, but you were right. Those tracks back there are the exact opposite of the one's Adam has left for years. It seems like a clever thing to do. Not many men would have ever realized that."

Adam spoke up, "Joshua, should I ride into town with the rest of you? I know that some bad things have been said about me and I have a feeling that some of them made their way west."

"Adam," I wasn't sure how to tell him, "You should come with us and we'll keep you at my place. To the rest of town, you are a stranger; they are all newer to the west than we are. Nobody is going to recognize you riding through town with us."

"He's right." Frank told Adam. "I wouldn't have known who you were out there at the cabin had you not told us."

William looked to the four of us; Turner, Frank, Adam and I, and said, "I'm going to take Mira home." We understood.

William rode away with Mira. Her folks must be worried by now. Frank told me that he would take Turner to the doc' to get his arm checked out. It didn't look too bad but you couldn't be too careful in the west. Adam and I rode on to the hitch rail in front of Louis' place. Instead of walking straight into the saloon, we walked to the café. We walked in and Dee looked up.

"Dee," I spoke softly but sure enough to let Dee know I was serious. "We got her, and another ally with all this trouble coming. William took her home to let her folks know she was safe."

Dee responded, "Good sheriff. I'm glad she's safe. I am more glad she's back to help me with these people's appetites."

I knew he was just making a joke and trying to lighten the mood. Dee seemed as if he too had seen his time behind a gun and he could tell we had had a rough day.

"Adam," I asked, "Have you eaten today?"

"Yes sheriff. You don't think I'd take an innocent girl on a ride out of town without taking some food for her to eat, do you? My father raised me better than that."

It occurred to me that Mira had mentioned the two of them eating. I was losing any doubt I may have had about Adam. He took a big chance doing all this and took very good care of Mira through the whole thing. I decided to get on with the day. I had a feeling at this point that trouble was coming soon and may turn out to be more than I had hoped for.

"Well, since you ate already and I know William is getting Mira home safe, you stay with Frank. I have to go to the office and speak to King Louis to see if anything happened at all while we were gone. Frank, make sure not to tell anyone who Adam is. We can use the help without everybody knowing yet."

I walked from Dee's to the jail to see if any letters or messages had been left. There was nothing new there. It dawned on me that I had let Dave go. I hope he listened and rode straight to the ranch. The old man would surely have some harsh words for him and let him know how foolish it was to take a swing at me. That would still be better than meeting the man that hired him and winding up like Matt. I knew there would be more death before all this was over, but I hoped it was the right men. I didn't need any more good men gone.

Next, I stepped from the jail to the boardwalk to walk on down to the depot to see if perhaps any wires had arrived. With all this trouble, I still had duties to perform. Before I could make three steps, I heard her voice.

"Joshua Mack," she almost sounded angry. "Joshua Mack, I need to know you are going to get through all this trouble and be with me when it is all done. I know you have a job to do and a town to protect, but I need to know." I had only heard that kind of emotion in Ms. Kitchen's voice one time before. It was the day she rode into town and told me about her father dying.

I spun around and looked at her. She was so beautiful. She was not too tall, not too short, and had the best shape and prettiest eyes I had ever seen. "Emily," I had only yet called her that a time or two before. "Emily, I am doing everything I can to protect this town, and you. I cannot promise that I will come through all of this without harm. What I can promise you, and have never meant anything more in my life, is if I am alive when this is over I will spend the rest of my days with you. I will hand this badge to another man, hopefully one that will keep us safe, and I will raise a family with you, if you don't mind."

A single tear left a trail down her cheek, as she smiled at me. "That's all I needed to hear. You find the men you and William are looking for and you kill them. Kill them so they can't harm anyone ever again!"

"All of this from a lady that won't sell guns or ammunition in her store. I don't believe I have ever imagined you speaking that way." I really didn't know she had it in her.

"Joshua, I still have the dreams, nightmares rather, of the day my father died. I don't like bad men. If all there were was good men or hunters in this world I would have no problem selling guns."

"Emily, I will do the best I can to give you the life you want. For the time though, I must try not to make too much contact with you until this is over. I don't want any harm to come your way."

She leaned in and kissed my cheek gently. She then understood fully what I was trying to tell her and turned and walked back to her store. I walked on to the depot, and as I walked that direction, I saw Frank taking Adam toward my place. He'd be safe there. This was one time I was glad to have help in the form of Sterling's son and my own blood.

When I got to the depot, the older man that had taken over the duties there was nowhere to be found. This was no surprise to me. He came and went as he pleased, as long as he was around when the train came. I noticed a wire was coming in. I went to the telegraph to see if I could make out what was being said. It had just begun.

SHERIFF MACK…WE HAVE INFORMATION THAT TELLS US YOU HAVE TROUBLE HEADED TO DALSTON…THE PIKE GANG IS ON TRAIL TO YOUR TOWN…WE WILL SEND AGENT SOON…LUCK TO YOU…US MARSHAL WHITE.

CHAPTER XIX

What could this all mean? I know Charlie had been in and out of town for a while. Perhaps there was new information and they had no way to reach him. It wasn't easy to follow one man in the west. I had no feeling that this message was sent from anywhere close enough to expect help to arrive in time. I still had a job to do and it all fell on us to protect Dalston. The government wasn't likely to send in the cavalry to rescue a small town such as ours.

I left the depot and stepped into the street to see the afternoon stage arriving. All I could think at this point was, I hope no more trouble is on that stage. I had enough on my hands now. The driver brought the stage to a halt in front of the hotel that was situated between King Louis' place and the jail. The shotgun rider hopped down and immediately noticed the star on my chest. He walked straight in my direction.

"Sheriff, I got a notice that was sent to you from a small town between here and St. Louis. The law in that town said it was urgent that I get this paper in your hands."

"Thank you, sir. Did they say what it was about?" This wasn't the normal rider, but they changed stages all the time.

"No they didn't sheriff. That sheriff said that I was to get this in your hands as soon as I got to town. It was luck you were here in the street when we pulled up. If you don't mind, or don't have any more questions for me, I'd like to get a bite to eat."

I took the paper from the man and directed him to Dee's, where the rest of the passengers were already headed. I thought for a moment about reading it right then and there but decided to go into the jail. I had no intention of letting anyone see me reading something that a man thought was so important. I truly couldn't be careful enough. I stepped into the jail and sat on the edge of the desk and opened the paper. It was a list of members, along with sketches of each, of the Pike Gang. Apparently the gang had been through this town, been seen by enough folks to be known, and the law figured they were heading this way.

I put the paper in my pocket and left the office. I walked to Louis' to see how things went while we were out of town. I entered the saloon to see only a few regulars and Louis. He was behind the bar cleaning glasses for the night's crowd.

"Louis, how was the town while we were gone? Was there any trouble?" I had a feeling there must not have been or he would have told us when we rode back in.

"No, no trouble here. It's a good thing too because I was the only one around. That Charlie hasn't been anywhere to be found since you and the boys rode out. I almost thought he came out to watch your backs. Then I walked a little way out of town and saw that his tracks led north and I knew y'all had ridden west."

"He really hasn't been around? You say he rode north?"

"That's how I read it sheriff. Other than that, everything was normal around here. No trouble at all."

"Thanks Louis. I appreciate you watching over things." I knew, somehow deep inside, this man could handle his own if it came down to it. I needed to head out north and

173

see what was so important that Charlie had to leave Louis here alone to watch over the town. We had some good men in Dalston, but most of them didn't know all that was going on.

I walked out of the saloon to meet Frank face to face. "Frank, it's pushing four-o-clock. I have to ride north a bit and then circle back south. I won't be back until late."

Frank always did know when something was on my mind. "What's north first, and then tell me what's south."

I knew out of all the men in the world, Frank and William, were men I could always trust. "Louis said he hasn't seen Charlie since we all rode out. He said he rode north. I'm just going to check on him. Dave, the man I let go from the jail this morning, was to meet the man that hired him to harm me at six where the river bends down on the sterling place. I was hoping to see who it is we are dealing with."

Frank looked a little upset. "It's not like Charlie to leave when he knew he may be needed."

I really didn't want to tell him about the wire I got from the other Marshall or the poster that came on the stage. Frank had said Charlie was his friend for years. Until I had this all figured out, I never wanted to put any doubt in his mind. "I'll be back shortly after dark Frank."

"Adam is at your place getting a little rest. I will keep an eye on things and I'm sure William will be back from taking Mira home soon. Be safe Joshua."

I knew Frank would take care of things. I also knew he would have given anything to go along with me. I walked

174

over to the rail where the big black was tied. I had not taken the shotgun from its scabbard since we went out earlier. It now made me feel better to have it with me as I rode out of town.

I had only ridden about three or four miles out when I saw a big man approaching. He didn't seem to slow up or be worried about who it was he was riding toward so I continued on. When I got close enough, I could tell it was Foster Grant, the man Pike claimed to work for.

"Mr. Grant, how are you?" I spoke as if nothing was wrong.

"Joshua Mack, I was headed into town to see Louis, and to find you. I wanted to see Louis for his whiskey. I've known him a very long time, since he was in St. Louis. I needed to speak to you about Pike."

"You've known Louis that long?" I didn't want to lead on to anything I was dealing with unless he had information for me. There was no reason to get him involved. He seemed to me to be a man just trying to push some cows.

"Yes sir," he smiled as he spoke. "I've known Louis a long time. He was once one of the best men I've ever seen in a fight. That's why he left St. Louis and brought his business here. The sheriff there, years ago when he had his saloon in town, had a son that thought he was untouchable because of who his father was. He came into Louis' place one day while Mary was still around and disrespected her. Louis drug the boy out in the street and beat him within an inch of his life. It was so bad that the doc' said one or two more punches would have killed the boy."

"Louis never mentioned any of that. Mary said something about some trouble and that was why they came to Dalston, but never Louis."

Grant spoke up. "It's good that you have him on your side. He outdrew that sheriff and just winged him enough to get out alive. He told the sheriff if anyone followed, he'd kill him and his son. Louis and his past were not why I came to see you Joshua."

"You said you needed to see me about Snake Pike. What is it you have to tell me about him?" I shifted around in my saddle, knowing I needed to get this meeting over with to get where I was going.

"I hired Pike because he is a hand with the cattle. It seems he is a better man with his gang behind him."

"You know about his gang, Mr. Grant? I received a wanted poster just before I left town with their pictures and names on it. I already knew about them, but I was hoping they would ride along with you and move past my town."

"I understand." Grant rolled a smoke as he spoke. "I just found out this morning. I rode out of camp to check on some cattle and the boys and followed his tracks to a place a ways from the herd. I got close enough to hear what he was saying. Well, not every word, but the part about wanting to kill you and your brother and take your town for all it is worth. He's still sore about the man in the hills taking that shot at him too."

"That's good to know Mr. Grant. We were already expecting his trouble, and we have more than him to worry about. Have you noticed any strange tracks around your

176

camp? The track I am looking for is a six on one side and a gun on the other." I hoped he could help me.

"I have seen those tracks, but they don't belong to any man in my crew. I can identify any of their shoes and those aren't like any I've seen." Foster Grant looked to the ground and finally peered back up from under his hat. "Does your brother really dump men in the Mississippi? I mean, is he really *the* William Mack? We have all heard the stories, but it has been thought for years to just be a legend."

"Mr. Grant, my brother is that legend. He watched our father get killed and it all began there. He is not a bad man. He's just had to do what he had to. I truly thank you for all the information and I hope you enjoy Louis' whiskey."

Just as Grant started to ride away, he turned back and said, "Be safe sheriff. I have never been through your town before but, I have never met a better sheriff. I'm sorry I brought Pike and his kind of trouble your way. The rest of the boys and I will move our herd around your town and head south tomorrow. Pike said something about being busy around noon tomorrow. I'm not sure what he meant, but I must move on when I can. I'm sorry I can't be of more help to you."

I continued riding north. I was glad to know that Grant knew what he was dealing with. Now, I also knew that possibly tomorrow around noon, I would have to deal with Pike and his gang. I wasn't sure if this had anything to do with the man that had the shoes similar to Adam's, or if it had anything to do with the man Adam and William had followed for so long. At the time being, I had to get on the trail to see what Charlie was up to. The wire I received earlier and the fact that he left not long after we rode out of town, both led me to wonder what Charlie was doing. Did he have an idea of what was going on? In my mind, there was only one way to find out. I had to see where he was headed.

CHAPTER XX

I left the worn trail heading north, knowing that Charlie would never follow the same trail that Grant, or anyone else, would take. I had ridden about another mile, through the brush and open fields of Missouri, and picked up Charlie's tracks. He was going somewhere in a hurry. I followed the tracks, stopping a time or two to check the trail and my back trail, for any sign of anyone besides Charlie. It wasn't long before I rode around a small hill and met up with Charlie.

"What are you doing here," Charlie said as if I had startled him. "Why are you out here when you had that trouble with Mira to go handle?"

"Hello, Charlie. It's good to see you too." I didn't want to let on any more than I needed. I wasn't sure what was going on but I had a feeling that some backhanded things were happening.

"Joshua," he spoke with a bit of surprise to see me. "Why are you out here? Didn't you and William and Frank go to get Mira?"

"Yes we did. You didn't expect us back so soon?"

"I just didn't know there was any place out west of town that was close enough for someone to hold up."

I thought about my next words carefully before I spoke. "You don't know about the cabin Charlie?"

"No, sheriff, I don't. What cabin?"

"Never mind, Charlie, why are you out here?" I didn't have time to waste anymore after stopping to talk to

Mr. Grant. I had to have answers and get south to see who was responsible for trying to pay men to take me and William out.

"I was just out for a ride. What are you doing out here?"

I knew well that he was trying to hide something, but I didn't know what. "I needed to ride out and see Foster Grant to find out when he was bringing his herd through town to sell. I know a few people that would love to have some fresh beef." I wasn't sure if he was going to buy what I was selling, but I was selling.

"Well he doesn't have much left in the way of good stock , but I guess beef is beef. Did you get to see Mr. Grant?"

I had a feeling he was trying to figure out some things of his own. "I saw Foster and we worked things out, Charlie. Why did you leave Louis alone to watch over the town? What was so important that you had to leave my town attended by one man, while the rest of us went out to get a girl?" I knew at this time that I had hit a nerve with him.

"Well sheriff, I didn't sense anything going on there and rode out of town to look into something of my own. If you don't mind, I need to get back now to see Frank."

"I don't mind at all, Charlie. You ride back and see Uncle Frank. If you think for one second that he won't tell me whether or not you came to see him, you're wrong. Blood is blood and water is water."

Charlie seemed as if he'd been hit square in the nose at that point. He acted like he didn't know how to act. "I will see you back in town sheriff. I hope whatever trouble is coming to Dalston, it doesn't catch you by surprise."

I wasn't sure how to take those words. "What exactly do you mean, Charlie?"

"Sometimes when troubles come, you don't even realize it. Trouble can hit you like a rattler, Joshua. It can strike when you least expect it and catch you off-guard like a rattler." There was a sense of something wrong in Charlie's voice. I was in no position to accuse, so I didn't. I just knew from this time forward, I had to keep an eye on anyone that wasn't William or Frank or Louis.

I had no desire to ride back into town and then head south. I decided to head southeast and follow the river just around town. This would keep me from being seen in town. My path would also lead me right by my place so I could make sure Adam was safe. Seems I at least owe that to the old man after all the years he's been there for me since pa died and William left. I got within a hundred yards of my place, which was right near the river, furthest from town. I saw Adam's horse in the corral so I stopped the black near the trough so he could drink. No need to tie him up, this was home.

"Adam," I announced myself. I surely didn't want to take a bullet from a guest as walked into my own house.

"Is that you, sheriff?" he responded as he stepped out the door. "I really like this place you have here. I always did like being near the river when I was young. It's a shame we never got to know each other as boys."

"Things work out the way they should and we can get to know each other in the future. Your father has sure been a huge help to me." As we spoke, I poured myself a quick cup of coffee before I had to go.

"Well Joshua, the old man speaks very highly of you. I know now is not the time, and I hope all this will be over soon, but I sure can't wait to see him." Adam definitely had an intense way about him that even showed through in his words.

"Adam, I was just stopping by. I still have somewhere to be before supper time. If I'm not back, most folks eat down at the café."

I poured the grains from the bottom of my cup and put it back on the table near the stove. I turned to walk outside and heard Adam say, "Be safe sheriff." I could tell he meant it too.

The black had his drink and was ready to ride. The next hour or so of the day could very well be the worst. I was riding downriver to a place where the river bent hard to the west. I was riding to check on the identity of a man that could be anybody. All I knew was he was a killer and I could not be too careful. If this man would kill Matt the way he did, he'd certainly kill me, if given the chance. I was planning to do my best not to give him that chance. I just hoped Dave took my orders to ride back to the ranch and stay put.

As I approached the bend, I dismounted from the black and loosely tied him to a branch on an old tree. From here I would need to be on foot. I spotted no tracks, which made me feel as if I had come the safe way. I was just thinking that this man would not approach the spot he told Dave to meet him from the east. It wasn't easy to get to the small clearing from the side of the river, not to mention it was hard enough to ride next to a river that big. The Mississippi has its way of intimidating and humbling men. I crawled to the spot I knew I could overlook the little meadow. It seems it was just as I remembered it from when I used to hunt a deer or two when I worked on the ranch.

It didn't take long. I looked at my watch and saw the man approaching around fifteen to six. It figured he would want to be in place when Dave rode up to collect. From my hiding spot, and with where I tied my horse, he couldn't have guessed I was around. The only problem was I couldn't make out who he was. Just that he was a big man. I would have liked to get a better look but, to put myself in a position to be in a gunfight with a man I knew nothing about and that no one really knew where I was other than Dave, who I had told to stay away, would just be foolish.

The big man pulled his watch from his vest pocket and checked the time. He had already gotten off his horse and was in position to cover the entrance of the clearing. Just as I was hoping he would give up on Dave showing, and ride away, another horse came riding in. I wasn't sure until the man spoke, but as soon as he did, I knew I was going to have to get closer and try to help.

"Dave," the man said and fear for Dave ran clean over my entire body. Why would a young man take this chance? I was crawling into position to be much closer when I heard Dave speak.

"You sure sent me after one tough man. That sheriff in town is hell to be reckoned with."

The big man responded, "Your face tells that story son. Did you even do any damage to him, or did you just get whipped?" There was something familiar about the way he spoke but I couldn't place why.

"He did all the damage," Dave said. "I got one swing and he took care of me like he'd been fighting his whole life. Are you still gonna pay up?"

"Oh, I've got something for you." As he said the words, his hand was reaching for his gun and he was fast. Dave had no chance. From my spot, I could only hope to get lucky or at least scare the man away. Dave went down as I fired. The man spun on his heel and fired in my direction but the bullet sailed over my head. He could waste another ten shots and not know exactly where I was. He rushed to his horse to clear out. As he rode away from the meadow, I fired a few more his way to make sure he wouldn't take the chance on circling back. I was reloading just in case and on my way to Dave's side. I knew he was hit by that shot. I just wasn't sure how bad.

"Dave, are you okay?" I was running to him. I could hear the big man's horse riding further and further away.

"I think so sheriff. If you hadn't fired when you did, I think he'd have finished me off but as it is, he got me in the side. I think I may be okay though," he was saying as he tried to get to his feet. He was to his knees when I got to his side. He was hit in the side but it didn't look too bad, other than losing a bit of blood.

185

"Here you go Dave. Put this handkerchief on there and I'm going to go get the black. I ran up over the little spot where I had been watching from and got my horse. It wasn't easy to lead him through the brush but I got him there and helped Dave up on his horse. I wasn't too worried about his wound; I had seen men live through much worse. I still wanted to get him to the ranch safely and get that gunshot tended to.

We were riding out of the clearing and heading toward the ranch house when Dave finally spoke again.

"Joshua, I didn't mean to cause you any trouble. I know I told you I'd go to the ranch but when you told me about Matt, I just got mad. I told the old man I was going to check on the cattle and rode out to meet him. I had no intention of getting paid. I just wanted revenge. I had no idea that big man was so fast."

"He was fast. I know he is at least part of the trouble we have coming to Dalston. I'm glad he wasn't luckier with that shot. We need to get you to the ranch house and get you patched up. Clint is the best patch man I've ever seen short of a real doctor."

"I'm sorry sheriff. I didn't mean to get shot."

"Nobody ever does, Dave. I wish I could say there wasn't more to come but there is."

We rode into the ranch yard to wave at a few of the hands smoking in front of the bunkhouse. When we got to the front porch, I expected Samuel to appear, but he was nowhere to be found. The old man stepped out of the house and looked straight to the bandage on Dave's side.

"Dave," the old man was stern. "If Joshua tells you the sky is green, you better by God believe him. I would have given you the money to keep you from riding out there."

Dave looked to the old man, then, to me, then, just stared at the ground before he answered. "Sterling, I didn't ride out there for the money. I was mad clean through that man had killed Matt. I was hoping to get a little revenge and save the sheriff here some trouble. It seemed obvious he had it in for Joshua and for William."

"Well," the old man said in a gentler voice, "Come on in and we can get Clint to look at that leg. Joshua, will you go to the bunkhouse and get him?"

I walked to the bunks and found Clint. "Tucker, we got a man that needs a little stitching in the main house."

"Well hello Joshua. What are you doing here and who's hurt? Is everything fine?"

"Everything is fine, Clint. Dave didn't listen to me and he rode out to meet the man responsible for killing Matt. Had I not been there, trying to figure out who the man was, he would have finished Dave off too. Seems this man, whoever he is, is very fast. My shot took his attention from Dave and Dave got away with one low down in his side. He should be okay but still needs patching."

"I'm on my way." Clint spoke as he stood up and gathered his bag of supplies.

We walked across the yard to the main house and found Dave, laid on a table. The old man must have told him to lie there. I made sure that he was going to be fine and told the men I had to get back to town. Sterling knew Dave was in good hands with Clint and walked me out. I was about to step off the porch and mount up when the old man spoke.

"Who is this man, Joshua?"

"I wish I knew," I really did. "I wish I knew and I was doing my best to find out. It was dusk and I didn't have any way to get close enough. Then Dave showed up. I did learn it was indeed the same man that killed Matt, and the same man that shot at William, Frank, Turner, Adam and I this morning, when we rode out west of town to get Mira back." I knew as I spoke the words, I was wrong for mentioning it.

"Did you say Adam?" The old man got real curious and serious real fast. "Do you mean my Adam?"

"I'm sorry Sterling, but yes it is your Adam. He is in town at my house right now. He is the man that took Mira and left the note for us to come get her. He looks well."

"I must go see him!" He meant it too.

"You can't. At least not right now, he needs to lay low with no one knowing who he is. Trust me, Mr. Sterling, he is good and he is right where he needs to be for now."

The old man got angry with me. I hadn't seen him truly angry in a long time. It had been since I worked for him.

"Damnit, Joshua, he is my son! I want to see him and I will! You have no right to keep that from me!"

I really didn't know how to respond to that. I knew he wanted nothing more than to see his son, but I thought he was better off in town at my place where nobody knew him. I still wasn't sure about Adam's past and needed him with me in town.

"Please listen, old man. I know he's your son and you've been worried and wanted him by your side for a long time. I just met him this morning. If you will remember, he was sent east before I ever hired on out here. He told me he got involved with some shady men there. He said that he had won a lot of shooting matches in the ranges they have in the cities there. He told me when he won so many he had every horse he has owned since, shoed the same. They all have a Six on one side and a gun on the other. It is designed so if anyone is following Adam, they read six-gun. He said it was a warning to them."

"Is he a good man, Joshua, like you?" Sterling sounded very sincere. I knew he understood what I was trying to say and that I had his best interest in mind.

"He is a decent man. You should be proud old man. He seems to have grown up in a very different place than we did, but he doesn't seem that different from us. He told me this morning that the people from back east wanted him to come back and take the ranch from you. Adam left soon after and never looked back. He also didn't think these people would ever find him here. He's been gone from New York for at least five years and said he came out west to get away from them."

"Who are these men Adam is trying to get away from?" Mr. Sterling was obviously very concerned. He wanted answers, but had plenty of questions too.

"I'm not sure," and I really wasn't. Then a thought occurred to me. "Where is Samuel?"

"He has been gone for a while Joshua. He left earlier and hasn't been back."

"Was he here when Matt was killed?" I knew the question would upset the old man but I had to ask. If he was gone then and gone this evening, he could be the man I need to worry about now.

"Yes Joshua, he was here." The old man sounded confused. "He was here all day yesterday, right by my side. You don't think he is involved in all this mess do you?"

"I'm not sure. All I know is that if he was here then he couldn't have been the man that killed Matt. That leads me to think he was not the man there tonight trying to kill Dave. If he is not the man I'm looking for, where is he?" I was doing my best not to confuse the facts or upset Mr. Sterling.

"I'm not sure. You know how things work out here on my place. If I hire a man to look after things, or do any job for that matter, as long as he does his job I leave him be. I treated you the very same way and you were the youngest I ever hired."

"I remember you were always fair about letting a man do as he pleased, as long as the work got done. It's just struck me odd that he wasn't here with it pushing dinner time." The last thing I wanted to do was to give the old man

190

any reason to worry. "Listen, Sterling, I'm not trying to accuse Samuel of anything. I just need to know who stands where in all this mess. I need to get back to town before William or Frank get worried."

"Samuel seemed like a straight shooter to me, but I understand your concern. You take care getting back to town and please keep Adam safe."

CHAPTER XXI

I rode into town on the main trail from Sterling's place. I saw no sign of Samuel, or any tracks other than my own and various random tracks from earlier in the day. This was the time of day that most people were either home or headed there for dinner. It was also the time that some went to Dee's to eat a good meal or to Louis' to have a little beef and beans, if he had it, and start a night of drinking. I noticed as I rode down the main street that William's and Adam's horses were at the saloon already. They were probably telling stories of how William had followed Adam, as he followed someone else. Frank's horse was tied up, with a few other random ones in front of Dee's. He always enjoyed the fare at Dee's more than what he could get to eat at Louis'.

I pulled up and tied the black to rail in front of the jail and walked to Dee's. I needed to see Frank after the meeting with Charlie. He looked up and waved me over to his table as soon as I walked in.

"Where have you been Joshua? You almost had William coming out to look for you."

"I had to ride north, because that's the way Charlie went soon after we left town to go get Mira. I needed to know what he was up to. On the way, I came across Foster Grant, the man in charge of the herd."

Frank always had a way of addressing one thing at a time. He started with my mention of Mr. Grant. "I saw Grant ride into town earlier and go to Louis'. Can't say I blame him. A man on the trail needs some good whiskey now and then. What did he have to say?"

194

I explained what Grant had said about Snake Pike and that he and the rest of his boys would be moving on soon. I then remembered the paper in my pocket with the pictures of all the men in Pike's gang.

"Joshua, this is better than them coming in here and us not knowing who they are. Now tell me," I could tell he'd been working out his words in his head. "What is your curiosity with Charlie?"

I didn't know how to tell Frank that I had a few doubts when it came to his friend of twenty-odd years. "I received a wire earlier today from the Marshal's office that they had information that the Pike gang was headed toward us. The wire said something about them sending an agent soon. Why would they send a wire like that if they knew Charlie was already here? It just didn't add up to me Uncle Frank, especially seeing as how he left Louis alone to protect the town while we were gone."

Frank had a tone in his voice. It wasn't meanness or anger. It was more like confusion. "Joshua, with the state of things around here, you are wise to be cautious of anyone or anything short of family. It certainly doesn't add up and, I have yet to see Charlie since we all got back this afternoon. I will keep an eye out and try to help in any way I can."

"Thanks Frank. I think I'll just go to Louis' and join William and Adam." As I said those very words, a man walked through the door. He was a stout looking man and I knew immediately I had seen him somewhere, recently. I just couldn't recall where. Frank had noticed the same man. Then he placed him.

"Joshua, that is that man Gentry, that Louis had to whip and run out of town. I saw him on my way back in after the meeting with the herd. Louis told me about him that evening. I'm sure it is him."

"I was trying to place the face, but now that you say it, it is him." As we were speaking, Gentry was checking out the room and crossing straight toward our table.

"Sheriff," he said as he glared at the badge on my chest. "I figured you to be in the saloon by now."

"Why's that, Gentry?" I replied calmly as I took a sip of the coffee Dee had brought me.

His hand was nowhere near making a move for his gun, so I wasn't too worried. "I just thought you'd be in there with your brother, enjoying the last night he will be alive."

Now that there was a direct threat but I tried to remain calm, like pa and William had always taught me. I wasn't sure what he meant or how he played into all of this, but I intended to find out.

"Last time I saw you Gentry, you were riding out of town with a whippin' written all over your face. I guess that explains why you didn't go in the saloon. You didn't want Louis to show you the err of your ways again." As I said it, Frank snickered a little. It ran all over the man standing over our table.

"Tomorrow, I will take care of that bartender, and I will take care of some more unfinished business! That is a promise, sheriff."

At that, I stood to face Gentry. "You wouldn't be making a threat here in my town would you?"

"I said it's a promise. I mean that. You all have trouble coming tomorrow and there's no way you can stop it. I'll see you then, sheriff." He turned and walked out the door and mounted up to ride out of town.

"Well, we know one we will have to deal with now. I wonder if he's tied in with the rest of this." Frank was thinking the same way I was.

"I'm going to go see William and Adam. Will you be around in the morning, Frank?"

"I wouldn't miss it Joshua. You, me, William and Louis against the world sounds like fun to me."

I left the café and walked down the road to the saloon. When I entered, I found the usual crowd, doing the usual things. I saw that the boys were at a table in the corner. They were at Frank's table, probably waiting on him to arrive. I crossed the room and asked the men to follow me to the bar. I wanted to speak to all of them, and to Louis.

We got to the bar and Louis excused himself from the man he was speaking to. He walked the length of the bar and came down to meet with us. I had to lay it all on the line. I knew that William was after a man for what he did to Maggie. I knew Adam just wanted to get back to the ranch and see his father. I also knew that I had Louis had Mary to think about. I was the only man of the group that was responsible for this town. I knew I needed help, but it's not easy to ask a man to stand beside you in the face of trouble.

"Listen, boys. We got trouble coming. The only thing I knew until tonight, over at Dee's, just before I came here, was that Pike and his Gang are headed our way. At the café, as Frank and I were talking, Gentry walked in."

"Did you say Gentry," Louis said. "You mean the man I put in his place for being rude to Ms. Kitchen?"

"Yes, Louis, I mean that man. That's not the worst part. He said tomorrow he'll take care of you, and some more unfinished business. I'm not sure what exactly he is talking about, but he meant it."

Louis turned three shades of angry red. "Let him come! Let him come and whatever his business, it won't be taken care of because he won't get past me!"

William spoke up. "What else have you learned? We haven't seen you since we all got back to town."

"Louis, I rode north and found Charlie. I'm still not sure what he meant by the things he said, or why he left you here in town alone. On my way though, I met Foster Grant on the trail."

"Isn't that the man that has that herd north of town?" William asked.

"Yes it is. He said he was headed in to see Louis. Was he here?"

"He came in and had one or two drinks and took a bottle with him. He seemed nice enough."

"Well, he told me that he found out about Pike's plan and he cut him loose. He said that he and the rest of his men would be heading through tomorrow to sell off his cows. It seems Pike is part of our trouble."

All of a sudden, I had a thought. "What happened to Turner? Why isn't he here?"

Adam replied, "He showed up at your house as I was leaving. He said he needed some rest and I figured you wouldn't mind, so I left him there and came to town."

"That's a good place for him. I know he wasn't shot bad, but he could use the rest. I think we need all the help we can get tomorrow. Frank said he'll meet me first thing in the morning. You can always count on him drinking coffee at Dee's as soon as the doors open." I was trying to get everything out in the open. I hoped I hadn't left anything out.

Adam finally spoke up. When he spoke, he sounded much like his father giving orders at the ranch when I was younger. "We know half the story. The other half, we can figure out tomorrow. I say we all get some rest and settle this then."

"That sounds good," I said. "I will be in town just after sunup. Thank you, men, for all sticking with me. I need to be getting home."

I walked away from the bar toward the door. I heard a man at the poker table yell loudly, "There's plenty of room in the Mississippi!" I knew it wasn't William's voice and I didn't recognize who it was. I turned to see a young man looking across the table at the dealer with his pistol drawn. I was going to step in and stop this kid from making a huge mistake, but before I did William was at the table himself.

"You think that's wise, son?" William was at the side of the table looking the kid dead in the eyes. "I'm not your kid, mister," he yelled. "This ain't none of your business."

"I think it is. You see son, you're quoting a legend. The legend of a man that is very good with a gun. Maybe he isn't the best, but so far, he hasn't been beat. That man doesn't like having to shoot men that try him all the time. It's no fun killing someone you've never even been properly introduced to."

William's words had taken a little of the edge off the kid, but the kid had not taken his gun off the dealer. I was slowly making my way across the room, and perhaps I was the only man moving at all. William at that point had had enough. The young man's gun was on the dealer and his eyes were on William. William dropped his hand to his holster and had his Colt pointed at the boy before any man in the room could even blink. I swear I even heard a few gasps of disbelief in the room.

"By God son, I am William Mack. Don't make a mistake you won't even get the chance to regret."

Sweat rolled down the boy's cheeks and forehead. He nervously lowered his gun and started to apologize to the dealer. He then turned to walk out of the saloon, embarrassed but thankful he was alive. William turned to walk back to the bar. I could see that look in his eyes. He must have known he had just saved that boy's life. The look on his face was a story in itself. It told a story of pain and relief. I knew deep down he never intended to become the legend he was. William just did what he felt he had to when pa was killed. He never meant for kids all over the west to imitate him and get themselves killed. There was truly only one William Mack and I was glad he would be by my side tomorrow.

I left the saloon without saying another word. I noticed William had crossed to the bar and swallowed a glass of whiskey. I couldn't wrap my mind around what it must have been like for him over the years. I just wanted to get home and get a little rest before the morning came. I walked down to the jail where the black was. I walked inside to see if anything was left on my desk.

I entered the jail to find a note on my desk. It had no name or identification on it. It simply read:

Joshua,

Tomorrow this all ends. It will be the end of you and your brother and any man that stands with you.

I wasn't surprised at all in finding this. I simply left the letter on my desk and walked out of the jail. I got on the black and rode home. When I got there, and had the horse unsaddled and fed, I announced myself to the house. I knew it was my house but I didn't want to startle Turner. He stepped out of the front door, rifle in hand.

"Is that you Joshua?"

"Yes Turner, it is. May I come in," I said jokingly. Turner had a little laugh and went inside. I followed and he had a cup of coffee waiting on me.

"Sheriff, what's going on? I needed rest and came here but I know the day didn't end there."

"Well Turner," I had to sort through all of it in my mind. "All I can tell you is that tomorrow, and who knows when, the trouble should all come to a head. Gentry, a man that rode into town and was run out by Louis, for disrespecting Ms. Kitchen, is back. We aren't sure where Charlie, the U.S. Marshal, stands in all this. Foster Grant, the man with the herd outside of town said he and his men were pulling out tomorrow after selling what cows they have left. The problem there is, Snake Pike and his gang are heading our way.

"Did you say Gentry?" Turner looked a little puzzled.

"Yes I did. That's all we know about him is his name is Gentry. He's mad at Louis for giving him a whipping. Why do you ask?"

"It seems like I've run into a Gentry in the past, more times than once, almost like we were headed the same place. I can't place him without a face but I know I have heard the name time and time again. Sheriff, I'll be good by morning. I'll be by your side."

"Thank you Turner. We should get some rest. Frank and William and Adam said they would be ready in the morning." I was really glad I had any help in the matter, much less men like my brother, uncle, old man Sterling's son, Louis and Turner. I wasn't sure what or how many were headed our way, but I was sure I didn't envy them.

CHAPTER XXII

I woke in the morning to find an empty house. There was a cup on the table and a fire in the stove. I poured myself a cup of coffee and walked out to the porch. When I stepped outside, I found Turner sitting, enjoying his own cup of coffee.

"Morning, sheriff," he said. "I know we don't know each other very well, but I should tell you I try to wake every morning by sunrise. I enjoy a good sunrise. It means I lived another day and slept another night. It's like the beginning of something new."

I almost felt as if time had turned itself back a few days, and William was here with me again.

"My brother said something very similar to me just a few mornings ago. You couldn't be more like him." I was also thinking that I missed the days of stepping out on my own front porch to enjoy my morning coffee, without being surprised by someone sitting there.

"I have done my best to follow William as close as I could. After my father was killed, I had nothing else. I've been in some pretty bad situations trying to stay close to him. Since you mention it though Joshua, I have sat a few mornings, at a distance, and watched William watch the sun come over the horizon with a cup of coffee."

"I must tell you Turner," I was all wrapped up in thoughts of my brother now. I have looked up to that man since we were kids, and even more after pa died. "I couldn't think more highly of a man than I do for William. I am sorry for your losing your father but, you couldn't have followed a better man through this world."

We sat quiet for a while and both got up to get more coffee. We were in no hurry to get on with this day. I think we both knew what it had to bring.

"I fed the horses while the coffee was on," Turner finally said.

"Thanks Turner. I'm going to town and get on with the day. If I let this trouble change my routine, then the entire town will question what's going on. I've been heading into town every morning since I put this badge on, and folks are used to it." I really just wanted to make sure nothing was happening yet, and maybe say good morning to Emily one more time before all Hell cut loose.

"I won't be far behind you sheriff." Turner seemed to me to be a trustworthy and honest man. It was a shame how he had grown up but, I'd seen men with better up-bringing turn out a lot worse.

I threw out the last of my coffee and put my cup back inside on the table. My mind was going in too many directions. I knew if today was the day, I couldn't ask for any more help than I had. I walked out, tipped my hat to Turner, and saddled the black to ride into town. My horse was feisty, almost as if he knew what today was to bring.

I rode into town the same way I did every morning. Everything seemed normal, until I tied my horse at the jail and started my morning walk. I was headed to Dee's to see Frank, and I was really craving a good breakfast for once, when Mary came running up to me.

"Joshua," she was in a panic. "That gang rode into town this morning. I wouldn't have known who it was had they not stopped me and asked who owned the saloon. Of course, I told them that Louis did. They said if he wasn't there in thirty minutes to open the doors, they'd break them down and serve themselves. The man out front of the group said, 'Snake Pike doesn't wait on no man, lady.'"

"What did Louis do, Mary?" I tried to remain calm. William and pa always said to be calm.

"He was furious, but he said he would go open the saloon and wait on you to get to town. He said you would know what to do." She had finally settled a little.

"Mary, you make sure that you, Emily, and Mira stay safe and out of the way today. I feel like everything is coming to a head now." I was nervous and cautious and maybe a little scared. Everything weighed on my move. Everyone's life was in my hands.

"I will take care of the girls Joshua," she said. I knew if I needed a lady to take care of things, I could count on Mary.

I proceeded with my walk of the town. I wanted badly to go straight to the saloon but, I also knew it was me or William or Frank that the Pike gang would want. They had no idea that Louis was with us and I had no intention of walking into a trap. Louis was a smart man, and level-headed enough to keep things going until we could figure all this out.

"Good morning Joshua." It was the sweetest words I had ever heard and all I could think about was living through the day and hearing those words every morning for the rest of my life. I turned to see a face that was as sweet, if not sweeter, than the words that were just spoken.

"Good morning Ms. Kitchen. How are you?"

"I'm fine." She looked straight in my eyes to let me know what she was about to say was important. "Joshua, the trouble is already here."

"Mary has already told me. The only problem is that they are just a few of the men I must deal with." I was worried more than ever. I wanted her and Mira to be safe. I wanted the same for Mary too.

"The men at Louis' aren't what I'm speaking of." She tried to appear casual, like we spoke every morning. It was clear she didn't want anyone that might be watching to think she was warning me. To help things, I smiled at her and pointed at a few things around town, like I was describing something we had talked about before. As if she could read mind, Emily kept on talking, looking around town.

"There are men staged all around town. I don't know who they are. The man that threatened me, the one that Louis sent packing, stayed in town at the hotel and left early this morning to go have breakfast at Dee's. Charlie, the Marshal, has been from the saloon to Dee's and back. There's also another big man here in town. He got a room last night at the hotel, but hasn't left at all this morning. I will go now to get Mira and meet Mary at her house. You know Louis bought it because it was built like a fort. We will be safe Joshua. You try to get these good men you have by your side through this alive and you be safe too. Please."

"Yes ma'am." At that she turned to walk away and I stood for a moment to admire the woman I wanted. She knew it and I knew it. I just had to settle all this today and then I could have her.

I turned to walk to Dee's. On my way up the street, Turner rode into town. I was glad to see him. It was a heavy burden to think that if any man of us had to die today, I wanted it to be me. I did not want another man's blood on my hands. There was always the possibility that none of us would see this thing through. I was thinking on the way to Dee's, where Turner had gone straight to, that I still didn't know where Charlie stood in all of this.

I stepped in the door of the café to see Gentry immediately look up and note my presence. Frank was already done with his breakfast and was relaxing over a cup of coffee. Turner sat next to him, ordering food for himself. I knew Dee would bring me the same thing I always had when I came to the café for breakfast. I had to walk right past the table Gentry was seated at to get to Frank and Turner. He looked down at his coffee, as if the last thing in the world he wanted to do was speak to me.

I stopped and spoke in the lowest voice I had. "I know you're here for William. You still have the chance to ride out. I can tell you I have never seen you in action. I have seen William, recently. I have never imagined a man being that fast. There is only one man I know faster than him."

"Who might that be sheriff?" Gentry asked with true curiosity. He wasn't threatened in any way. He was here to do what he thought he needed to and there wasn't anything anyone could say or do to change that.

"The only man I know faster than William is here in town. He doesn't brag and he doesn't have a legend built around his name. He is just an ordinary man that happens to be fast and good with a gun." I wanted Gentry to think about what he was doing. If I could convince him to leave, that meant one less problem to deal with.

"You tell this man, sheriff, to come and see me when I am through with William. Now if you don't mind, I would like to finish my coffee and get where I need to be."

I had the feeling he wasn't the type of man words could run off. I decided to bring him up to speed on the events happening and about to happen here in Dalston. "Gentry, are you aware of the other men in town that are mixed up in all this mess?" I couldn't believe he actually responded to the question.

"Sheriff, I am aware that William is your brother. I am aware that Frank is your uncle. I am not sure who the man sitting with Frank is. None of you have anything to do with why I am here."

"Those aren't the men I'm talking about. There is a gang of men in the saloon right this moment that are here to run all over this town, as they please. There is also a few other threats that I'm not quite sure where they stand, but I anticipate they are enemies. Have you thought at all of these men?"

"I have only one thing on my mind sheriff. I came here to kill your brother. "

I wanted to whip this man right there and then. I knew if Louis had done it once, I could too. But another

209

thought came to mind. We may as well let this all turn out however it does and be done with it, for good or for bad, today. The last thing I wanted was to send Gentry packing with another shiner and to have him come back in a few days. I just wanted all of this to end. With that on my mind, I looked him dead in the eyes and walked away to join Frank and Turner. Our food was being brought to the table as I approached.

"Turner," I spoke as I removed my hat and sat down, "We are in for it today."

"I know, Joshua."

We ate in silence and I watched as Gentry left the café and crossed to the saloon. We got to the end of our plates of food and Frank finally spoke up.

"Tried to tell him to leave, didn't you?"

I had just finished breakfast and took a sip of coffee. "Yes Frank. He is the young boy that followed William all these years, and came here to kill him."

"Well," Turner said, "Good luck with that. I have never seen anyone as fast as William."

"I have." Frank watched Gentry walk to the saloon through the window as he spoke. He was as usual, always so casual about things.

"Who in the world could be faster than William?" Turner was shocked that anybody could even make such a statement.

Frank looked from the street to Turner. He let the question hang in the air for a moment before saying, "You'll find out today. I'm almost sure of it, son."

Turner left it at that and didn't press any more. We all enjoyed our coffee for a few minutes. I finally got up from my chair and told the men that I was headed to the jail.

"You be safe out there, Joshua," Frank said. "I'll be in place where you need me when everything goes down."

"I know, Frank. Turner, you be safe. It seems it will be a long day."

CHAPTER XXIII

I walked out the door of the café, stopping on the way to let Dee know to keep himself and his wife safe when everything started to happen. A man never wanted to get hit by a stray bullet. There's no use going down for another man's fight. For that matter, I didn't want any innocent people to be injured in the fight that was to come today.

I entered the jail to find William sleeping on my desk. It was a strange place to find my brother.

"What are you doing, William?"

"I needed the rest," he said as he cleaned away his eyes. "What's going on out there?"

"Well, William, Gentry is here and wants to kill you. He says that is all he came for."

"Who is Gentry?" William spoke as if he really had no clue.

"Gentry, as far as I can tell, was the boy whose father you killed years ago. He is not tied in with all the rest of the men we may have to face. He did leave the café and cross to the saloon where Pike and his men are."

"I wish he could understand that I didn't want to kill his dad. I shot him in the leg hoping he would give up. He didn't. Now I have to face his son. You said the Pike gang is in the saloon. I saw them ride into town and go there when Louis opened. I have also seen Charlie go from the saloon to Dee's and back to the saloon. I wondered what that was all about but I needed to get a wink or two."

"William, I know you came here for your own reasons. I hope we find out who it was that killed Maggie. After all this is done though, if we are both still standing, I hope you will stick around."

"I hadn't planned on it Joshua, but that Mira is the prettiest thing I've ever seen and she is worth staying for. We will both be standing when this is all done, brother."

I told William that Frank and Turner were at the café and I needed to go to check on Louis.

"Are you crazy, little brother? There are men in that place that are just waiting to get a clean shot at either of us."

"I know. That's why I am going straight there. I need to size up the odds and find out where we stand. Don't worry William. They will wait until everything is in place."

"I hope so Joshua. Give them all a message from me. Tell them 'There's plenty of room in the Mississippi!'" He meant it too. He wanted me to tell them that and he knew there would be bodies floating the river tonight.

I crossed the way to the saloon. It was possible I would never walk out these doors after they swung shut behind me. This was my town and I refused to let men come in and tell me where I could or couldn't go. I walked in like I didn't even see any of the men there. I did though. I think they were so caught off guard that they had no idea how to react. There were a few men at a table in the corner playing cards. They must've been some of Pike's gang. Pike and Gentry and Charlie were all standing together at the far end of the bar. They stopped talking long enough to notice me entering. I walked directly to the bar, where Louis appeared to be a little relieved that I had arrived.

"Get me a beer, Louis," I said as if I was just here for the beer. I had spoken loud enough so everyone could hear me.

Louis knew I didn't drink that early, but I knew he didn't usually open that early either. He knew I had just come to check on him and to see what we were dealing with. Louis got me my beer and I took a big swig as he spoke softly.

"There are seven total, including Pike, in his gang. Charlie seems to be bad. That man I whipped is just here for blood and has let the rest of them know that William is his. There is talk that the man behind Pike and his boys coming to our town, and the man that is tied in with Charlie, is to come to town soon. They talk as if he will be here before long."

"Thank you Louis. Are the girls safe?" I didn't want to linger too long. I just came to see where we stood.

"They are safe. Mary got them to the house."

I took a coin from my pocket and threw it on the counter. "Thank you, Marcus Thompson. Now take your shotgun from beneath the bar and keep these men from getting too nervous as I leave. Louis had the look of a man caught with his pants down. I had known for a while that he was the man on the poster from St. Louis. I just didn't believe him to be a crook and never was one to let another man form my opinions for me.

Louis spoke as he pulled the shotgun from beneath the bar and checked the shells. "I had the feeling you knew. I got a dirty break there. I appreciate you leaving me be. I got your side in all this trouble, Joshua."

I nodded and turned from the bar. I walked to the center of the room and stood as if to make a speech. I watched the men in the corner and knew that Louis had the double barrel trained on Charlie, Gentry and Pike. "If any man doesn't want to die, he needs to drop his weapon in the street and ride out of town. You are all facing a bad situation. I know you think you all have the numbers on us, but if you stay, you will die! I'm in no mood for arresting anyone." I couldn't detect a movement in the room. I know they figured to have such good odds that none of them were scared by my words. They had to know that men would at least be shot today, if not killed. They were all thinking it wouldn't be them. I left the saloon without looking back at any of them.

I walked out to the street and went back to the jail. I walked in to find William had left. It finally occurred to me that I had not seen Adam all morning. I was removing the badge from my shirt as he entered the jail.

"Why are you taking off your star?"

I laid it all out for him. The fact that everything would end today, that Charlie was dirty, that there were Pike and six more men with him in the saloon, and that Gentry was here and another man was to come. He would be the man in charge.

"I can't honestly wear that star today, Adam. I know it will come down to me killing men for reasons that may not have much to do with the law. Besides that, when this is all done, William and I, if we are both still standing, will put every one of them in the river. Today, I stand by my blood. I don't need a badge to do that."

"I understand, sheriff. I am here for my family too. Why don't you give me that star? I want a feeling that this is all legal. I will keep it in my pocket and it will help me feel right about anything that goes down today."

"Take it," I said as I scooped the badge off my desk and tossed it to Adam. "Let's go to the café and meet with William and Frank."

We stepped out of the jail, only to see old man Sterling and Clint riding up to Dee's. We walked over to the café to meet them at the door. Old man Sterling was looking at the man with me like he knew him. I gave him a sign and nodded to let him know he was right. We didn't need the boys in the saloon knowing who Adam was yet. The saloon; as I thought about it, I looked that way. I turned my head just in time to see a man walking in through the double-doors. He looked familiar, even from behind, but I couldn't quite place who it was. At least, not without a good look at his face.

We walked into the café to find Turner sitting alone at the table I had left him and Frank at. I asked Dee to bring some coffee to our table. I motioned for Turner to come join us, as Adam and I sat down with Sterling and Clint. I knew they hadn't come for breakfast. Sterling had the best cook in the state at his ranch and he cooked every morning, noon and night.

"You look good, son." The old man finally spoke to Adam.

"Thanks, Pop. I'm sorry we have to reunite on these terms. It is good to see you."

I interrupted for a moment. "Where is Frank, Turner? And, have you seen William?"

Turner looked up from his coffee. "Joshua," he spoke with an intensity I had seldom heard, "Frank said he would be in place when we needed him. William is right behind you."

I looked over my shoulder to find my big brother coming in to join us. He had two guns strapped on. I had never seen him wear two before. I glanced to his left hand gun and noticed it was much older than anything a man wore these days. It was pa's gun. He had that look in his eyes again. William was wearing the only thing either of us had left from our childhood, and looked like he was ready for war.

"William," I said as I shoved a chair out for him, "Join us."

"We don't have time for this Joshua. There are men in this town that need to be in the river. This is our town and we will not back down for anyone."

At his words, I stood and said, "William is right. We need to go take care of all of this business now. Adam, I want you to keep your old man safe and out of this."

The old man stood up as to object. He was beat to the point by his son. "I will not stand by and watch you go to war without me."

Instinctively, I grabbed Adam by the shirt collar and slammed him against the back wall of the café. "You owe me this! You are to take care of your father! William, Turner, Frank and I will handle the trouble outside these doors!" I was yelling the entire time.

Adam tried to plead his case. "I didn't come back here to watch other men fight a fight to save my town."

I wasn't angry with Adam. I just needed him to know. "This isn't your town. It hasn't been for a long time. This is my town. It is my girl and William's girl. I have been here the entire time you have been gone. Your father gave me a job when I needed one and has done as much for me as any man I've known. My father was killed and my brother had to leave town to keep trouble away from me. You stay with the old man and make sure he is safe. Do you understand me?"

Adam had finally calmed down under my grip and my words. "I know what you mean, Joshua. I'll stay with my dad and keep him safe." I knew by the look in his eyes, he knew what I meant. If we were to fall today, someone had to be there to keep the town, and Sterling's ranch, safe.

William and Turner followed me from the café. We headed to the jail. It was the strongest building I knew of in town. The second strongest was Louis' house. I prayed the girls would stay there and be safe.

CHAPTER XIV

We walked to the jail. I knew Frank was going to be somewhere, ready and in place, when everything went down. Right now all I could think was; I hope we all lived through this day. The girls were at Louis' house with Mary. Adam and Clint Tucker were at Dee's with the old man. Dee had mentioned getting home to his wife. Louis was in the saloon with who knows who. Turner, better from his shot to the arm, was here with William and I. I went directly to the gun cabinet and pulled a shotgun out. I checked the loads and tossed it to Turner.

"I want you to have that. William and I are better with our pistols. I'm not saying that you aren't good, but you aren't known. You holding that to start this whole thing off will make them think twice about going for you." I hoped I hadn't made a play toward his pride.

"No problem," Turner replied as if he were a soldier taking an order. "Whatever you think is best."

William spoke up. "What are we going to do?"

I got real serious, and to be honest, real mad. "We are going to clean this town out and throw all of them in the damn river when we're done! I've had enough of this! I will not tolerate men bringing trouble to my town."

As soon as my words broke off, I heard a voice from the street. It was Samuel's voice. I couldn't quite make out what he was saying through the thick walls of the jail, and the solid door. I walked over and cracked the door to be able to hear him out. As I cracked the door, it was pounded with bullets. It seemed as if a hundred men were firing at the jail. Turner flinched and moved to a corner across the room.

222

William looked me dead in the eyes, and I was glad he had that particular look. I guess I looked very much the same.

"Joshua, is there another way out of here," William was trying to talk over the shots.

I looked at him and Turner and told them, "Follow me. I put this exit in years ago and no prisoner I've ever had has figured it out. I guess they never thought there would be a way out of this building built into a cell. Thank goodness, huh?"

When we got to the back cell and I reached under the bunk to remove a panel, both men gave a little laugh. We slid through the hole under the bunk just as the shots at the front door stopped. I knew that anyone in town, or even new to town, thought there was only one way in or one way out of the jail. All I could think was I never anticipated having to use this hole. We got outside, just behind a woodpile I always kept stocked, and William looked at me for direction.

"What do we do now, little brother?"

"If we stay behind the building next to us," I said while gesturing toward it with my head. "We should be able to get out to the street and see who and how many we are dealing with. Whoever it is, they probably think we are hunkered down in the jail still."

"Sounds good Joshua," Turner said and the three of us started walking around the building.

When we reached the corner, there were three men standing in the street, facing the jail. We had moved far enough to be enough behind them to walk out on the street.

As we rounded the corner and were moving behind them, Turner made the perfect move. He had folded open the double-barrel, and as we approached the men, he whipped it up and it snapped closed. You could see the tension in all three men's bodies.

"Drop your guns, or die." I didn't want to give them the chance. Luckily, for them, they obliged and all dropped their weapons on the street and slowly turned around to face us.

William looked straight to Gentry and asked, "Do I know you from somewhere son?"

He replied, "You killed my father years ago and I came here to kill you. I don't have any other business with these men. I just came for you."

"You are the boy, aren't you? I had hoped you would grow up and realize your pa left me no choice that day. I really didn't want to have to kill you."

As William's words broke off, I spoke up. "Samuel, I had felt there was something wrong with you. Why are you doing this?"

"I met a young man named Adam years back and he was the best shot I've ever known. He said he would meet me here in Dalston someday to take over his father's ranch and the whole town with it. He left and headed west. If he was here now, you'd be in trouble though. He is the best I've ever seen."

"Not to take anything away from the boy, but fast or good in the East don't mean much to us here in the West.

Just so you know; Adam is here. He is at the café right now with his father, probably catching up on years of lost time." I wanted him to know he had misjudged young Sterling.

The third man standing before us was the hardest to see. It was Charlie. Turner took his chance speaking. "You, lawman, what are you thinking? Why are you here?"

"I came to take the ranch and the town too," Charlie said dryly. He was very cool about things and it worried me. I knew this was too easy. "You didn't think I wanted to be a Marshal my entire life did you? It's hell on a man when he can't lie in a bed under his own roof at night."

I had another question. "Which one of you killed Matt and tried to kill Dave?"

"That was me," Charlie said. "I couldn't risk them identifying me."

"That means you are the man with the six gun horseshoes."

Charlie replied, "Yes Joshua. Samuel told me all about Adam and I figured on pinning this all on him after it was over."

"That may have been a good plan if your shoes weren't the exact opposite of his."

Charlie smiled a little when he said, "It might work out to be a good plan after all."

The first shot whipped just over my head and took my hat off. William, Turner and I just cleared the edge of the nearest building as the rest of the shots rang out. The other three men in the street now had time to collect their pistols. The thought came to me.

"That's what Charlie meant. I should've known. With these men right in front of us, I forgot about Pike and his men. Charlie said sometimes trouble bites like a rattler."

Turner looked as if he knew what I was saying. "Snake Pike. Like a rattler."

William was angry. "They must have spread out on rooftops or buildings all over town. Now we're pinned down Joshua."

I felt at that moment that I had personally put my brother in a bad place. I had no idea how we would get out of this until I heard the boom. There was only one boom like that in this world. It was Uncle Frank's rifle. As we heard the noise, a man fell from the roof above us and was dead on the ground.

"Thought you could use a little help, boys," Frank yelled from the old hostler's barn on the hill at the end of town.

"Thanks Frank. We need it."

Another man poured out a window across from us. That was a loud shot too, but hard to place. Then we heard his voice. "I wanna play too," Louis yelled. "I figure, there are seven of that Pike gang, Frank. Bet I get more of 'em than you."

"You're on Louis. If you win, I'm buying tonight. If I win, drinks are on you."

William laughed a little. Before he could even get his words out, I think Frank and Louis had both shot another man. They had both yelled out the number two. "Here we are pinned down, and those two old men are making a game of it."

Turner had been peeking around the building and turned back to us. "They're still out there. It's like they are waiting on us."

I looked to William and Turner. "They think they have the numbers. They probably figure to let Pike get one or two of us, and then they can finish the job."

"They may think we have moved again," William said, "Especially after that trick you pulled getting us out of jail. It was kind of funny to see a sheriff breaking out of jail."

We heard Louis yell, "That makes three for me Frank. Looks like you are buying."

Another loud boom rang out and we heard Frank. "It's even Louis. Joshua, that makes six we've got so far. The only one left is Pike."

I looked at William and Turner and said, "I'm going back through the hole in the jail. Give me a minute or so and I'll meet you boys out front. It's time to end this!"

At those very words, William stood up and loosened the pistols in his holsters. It didn't take but a few moments for me to get back inside and to the front door of the jail. I

227

looked out to see the three men still had their attention turned to where William and Turner were. I saw William come around the corner with a pistol in each hand. I busted out the front door with a yell, hoping to get one or two of them to turn to me. William shot Charlie in the leg with his left-hand gun and the Marshal dropped his weapon. Gentry got one bullet into William's leg before he was hit by four shots from William's right-hand gun.

While all this was going on, my yell had drawn Samuel's attention. He used an old maneuver I had only seen once before. As he spun and drew, he was dropping to a knee. He would have got me too, had I not seen this move before. Instead, the one shot he got off went over my head, because I had also dropped down and put four doses of lead in him before he could fire again. Gentry was dead, and so was Samuel. I didn't even have time to ask William how bad he was hit. He walked straight over to Charlie, who was struggling to get to his feet. William acted as if he didn't even feel the bullet strike him. I could now see he was hit in the upper thigh.

He leaned down and picked up Charlie's gun. As he stood, he placed it back in the holster on Charlie's side. He then took five steps back. Turner and I had no clue what was going on.

"I remember seeing you in Denver a few years back. You were there weren't you?" Charlie looked up at William. He was scared. He had to know there was no way Pike was getting him out of this.

"I was in Denver." The next words to leave his mouth were to be his last. "I knew I had to have her and he didn't deserve her, the first time I ever laid eyes on Maggie."

William drew and shot what must have been every bullet remaining in both of his guns. Charlie never had a chance. The door to the café busted open and old man Sterling came out with Pike holding a gun to his back, hiding behind Sterling.

"Sterling, are you okay? Where are Clint and Adam?" I wanted no harm brought to the old man that had done so much for me.

"He came in through the back during all the ruckus and shot Clint. He knocked Adam over the head first and as Clint was drawing, he shot him. Clint won't make it, Joshua." The old man had sadness in his voice.

"Shut up old man," Pike yelled. "I'm taking you and getting out of town." He was backing away, looking for a horse, when I saw Adam for the first time since this whole thing had started.

Adam spoke as calm as any man I'd ever heard. "You aren't going anywhere."

Pike, at the sound of Adam's words, spun just in time to see the star on Adam's chest. Adam had three shots in Pike and was holstering his gun as Pike fell to the ground. "Are you good pa?"

Sterling turned to his son and replied, "I'm fine."

When I turned around to see Frank walking down the street from the barn and Louis coming out of a building up the way, William and Turner were already stripping the men of their personal things and any identification they might have had. Frank and Louis were arguing over who was to buy, since Adam had killed the seventh man. Sterling told the men he'd buy for everyone after the mess of bodies was cleaned up. That's when Louis let Frank in on the joke. He said, "Frank, it was fun but it wouldn't have mattered who got more of 'em. I own the place, remember?" Everyone had a good laugh at that.

I walked back to Adam and told him that star looked better on him than it did on me and that I thought he should keep it. This town needed a new sheriff anyway. Sterling and his son went into the café to get Clint's body. I figured they would take him to the ranch to be buried. Frank and Louis walked away to go tell the women everything was fine, and it would all be over after we finished cleaning up the street. After getting all ten of the dead men, aside from Clint, loaded on the backs of horses, Turner went to join the rest of the men at the saloon. William and I headed to the river.

"The river is running good today Joshua."

"Yes William it is."

"How did you get so good, little brother? That was a wicked move he used and would have beat about any man I know, fast or not."

"One of them Sloan boys got me in the shoulder that way, William. When I saw Samuel's knee give, I just knew to drop and fire."

We threw every last one of those men into the river, and were glad to be done with them. I had always wondered what it felt like.

"What now, William? Are you figuring on staying around?"

"I will be wherever my brother and Mira want me to be, Joshua. I saw you give Adam your star. What'd you have in mind?"

"Emily has her store and I have a little savings put up. I was thinking about maybe opening a ferry just down river." We were finally back to being two brothers standing on the side of the mighty Mississippi, watching the boats go by.

"Old Jack already has a ferry. He's been here running that thing since we were kids."

The two of us had turned and were mounting up to ride back to see our friends and our ladies when I responded to his comment.

"I thought about that William, but you should know as well as anybody, there's plenty of room in the Mississippi."

16630398R00123

Made in the USA
Lexington, KY
02 August 2012